U0094011

哈福

哈福

哈福

哈福

Easy American English

1分鐘快聽學習法

躺著學美語會話1000

用TED名師的方法，說一口道地美國話

張瑪麗, Willy Roberts ——合著

哈福

全方位自我表達‧馬上學馬上用

　　各位親愛的讀者，想必都期待著口若懸河地說英語。無庸置疑地，你絕對辦得到！

　　在學英語的過程中，你可能遇到這些困擾：

● 每次想用英語交談，明明腦中已想好完整的句子，卻無法流暢地說出口。

● 和老外相處時，學過的句子好像都忘了，不知道該如何打開話匣子。

● 講話時，遇到一個生字或不知道該如何說的一句話，當場楞在那裡，真是有口難言。

　　為什麼學了一輩子的英文還是開不了口？

　　以目前的教育制度來說，一個學生若從國中開始學英文，到大學畢業為止，少說也有十二年，花了這麼多時間去學習英文，最後的結果，卻是什麼也沒有，面對老外，依然張口結舌。

　　為什麼？想必是學習方法或學習教材有問題吧！

　　有鑑於此，本書才應運而生，讓學英語的中國人，能夠找到一條學英語的捷徑，是您突破會話障礙最好的一本會話書。一般人學習英語多年，還不會應用，不敢開口，本書讓您重建信心，把英語說得和母語一樣好，講一口生

動活潑的英語,在短期內發揮十足的潛力。

本書最大特色是:

- 用最 Easy 的單字,說最簡單的英語,重建你學好英語的信心。
- 精選最常見的會話場景,迅速掌握正確的表達方式。
- 不必死背,就可以生動、明白地將意思說出來。
- 融合美國文化,句型解說生動,一學就上手。
- 套用句型公式,文法自然融會貫通。
- 配合常用例句,單字不用背,自然記得多、記得牢。

如此一來,無論在考試、職場上或與老外聊天,您都可以行遍天下無敵手,溝通無國界。

真的!學英語可以很輕鬆,只要掌握簡單單字、簡單會話,同時配合美國專業播音員錄製的 MP3,循序漸進、每天反覆學習,絕對可以擺脫遇到老外說不出三句半的惡夢。

凡事起頭難,學英文也是如此,只要突破剛開始的困境,最後一定能夠苦盡甘來。

CONTENTS

Chapter 3

社交英語 **57**

Chapter 4

飲食英語 **67**

Chapter 9

保健英語 143

Chapter 10

休假英語 157

Chapter 11

租屋英語 173

Chapter 12

資訊英語 187

Chapter 13

科技英語 201

Chapter 1

見面的英語

Unit 1

How are you today?
你今天好嗎？

A Hello John.
哈囉，約翰。

How are you today?
你今天好嗎？

B I'm fine.
我很好。

A Have you finished writing your paper?
你的研究報告寫完了嗎？

B Yes. I finished it this morning.
是，我今天早上把它做完了。

▶ 對話二

A I just made some coffee.
我剛泡了一些咖啡。

Would you like some?
你要不要喝？

B Yes. Thank you.
好，謝謝你。

A How do you take your coffee?
你要怎麼喝？

12

B I take mine with cream and sugar.
我的咖啡要加糖和奶精。

純美語解說

喝咖啡時，有人要喝加糖或奶精的咖啡。有人要喝不加糖或奶精的咖啡，這種不加糖或奶精的咖啡叫做「black coffee」。如果你要拿咖啡請對方喝，你想問他要喝加糖或奶精的咖啡，還是喝不加糖或奶精的咖啡，英語的問法就是「How do you take your coffee?」。你也可以問他說「Sugar and cream?」，意思就是問他要不要糖和奶精。

會話靈活練習

▶ 問對方要不要去看表演

A Are you going to see the play tonight?
你今晚要去看表演嗎？

B Not tonight.
今晚不行。

I have to study.
我得讀書。

▶ 問對方何時要出去旅行

A When are you travelling to Boston?
你什麼時候要去波士頓？

B Next week.
下星期。

關心對方

A You look tired.
你好像很累。

B I didn't get much sleep last night.
我昨晚睡得很少。

邀約對方去看電影

A Are you coming with us to the movie?
你要跟我們一起去看電影嗎？

B Yes. Just let me get my coat.
好，我去拿件大衣。

問對方修幾門課

A Do you have a lot of classes this semester?
這學期你修很多課嗎？

B Yes. I have a full load.
是的，我的課排得滿滿的。

英語會話單字

☑ finish   ['fɪnɪʃ]   完成

☑ paper   ['pepɚ]   （學校的）研究報告

☑ coffee   ['kɔfɪ]   咖啡

☑ cream   [krim]   （喝咖啡用的）奶精

☑ sugar   ['ʃʊgɚ]   糖

☑ travel   ['trævl]   旅行

☑ tired   [taɪrd]   疲倦的

☑ semester   [sə'mɛstɚ]   學期

☑ full   [fʊl]   排滿的

☑ load   [lod]   工作量

Unit 2

My name is John.
我的名字是約翰。

▶ 對話一　　　　　　　　　　　🔘 MP3-03

A Hello. My name is John.
哈囉，我的名字是約翰。

B Glad to meet you.
很高興見到你。

I'm Mary.
我叫瑪莉。

A I just moved here recently.
我最近才搬來的。

B Where are you from?
你從哪裡來的？

A I'm from Taiwan.
我來自台灣。

▶ 對話二

A Hi. My name is John.
嗨，我的名字是約翰。

I'm in your History class.
我跟你同一班歷史課。

B Hi. I'm Mary.
嗨，我叫瑪莉。

A What do you think of our professor?
你認為我們的教授怎麼樣？

B I like him.
我蠻喜歡他的。

He's very interesting.
他很風趣。

純美語解說

不管在任何場合，你想跟對方認識，你可以走過去先自我介紹，再問對方的姓名。做自我介紹的句型有兩個，一個是「My name is ＋你自己的名字 .」，另一個句型是「I am ＋你自己的名字 .」。

彼此介紹過姓名之後，如果你要問對方從哪裡來的，英語句型也有兩個，一個是「Where are you from?」，另一個句型是「Where do you come from?」；要回答這個問題，回答的句型也有兩個，一個是「I am from ＋你來的地方 .」，另一個句型是「I come from ＋你來的地方 .」。

會話靈活練習

▶ 自我介紹，並問對方的名字

A Hello. I'm John.
哈囉，我叫約翰。

What's your name?
請問你的大名？

B My name's Mary.
我叫瑪莉。

▶ 自我介紹，以便與對方認識

A Hello. I'm John.
哈囉，我叫約翰。

B Glad to meet you.
很高興認識你。

My name's Mary.
我叫瑪莉。

▶ 自我介紹，以便與對方認識

A Hi. My name's John.
嗨，我的名字叫約翰。

B Nice to meet you, John.
約翰，很高興認識你。

I'm Mary.
我叫瑪莉。

▶ 與鄰居打招呼

A Good afternoon.
午安。

I'm your next door neighbor.
我是你的鄰居。

B Pleased to meet you.
很高興認識你。

告訴對方，你是新到任的秘書

A Hi. I'm the new secretary.
嗨，我是新秘書。

B A pleasure to meet you.
很榮幸認識你。

英語會話單字

☑ move	[muv]	搬家
☑ recently	[ˈrisn̩tlɪ]	最近地
☑ history	[ˈhɪstrɪ]	歷史
☑ professor	[prəˈfɛsɚ]	教授
☑ interesting	[ˈɪntərɪstɪŋ]	有趣的
☑ meet	[mit]	見面
☑ next	[nɛkst]	下一個
☑ neighbor	[ˈnebɚ]	鄰居
☑ secretary	[ˈsɛkrəˌtɛrɪ]	秘書
☑ pleasure	[ˈplɛʒɚ]	秘書
☑ next door		隔壁

Do you have the time?
你知道現在幾點嗎？

▶ 對話一   💿 MP3-04

A Excuse me. Do you have the time?
對不起，你知道現在幾點嗎？

B Yes. It's twelve o'clock.
知道，現在是十二點。

A Thank you.
謝謝你。

Do you know when the bus will arrive?
你知道公車幾點到嗎？

B It should be here in fifteen minutes.
應該再十五分就會到。

A Thank you.
謝謝你。

▶ 對話二

A Would you mind if I sit with you?
你介意我坐你旁邊嗎？

B Not at all.
不介意。

A What do you think of the food here?
你認為這裡的食物怎麼樣？

B It's all right.
還好。

純美語解說

「Excuse me.」這句話中文翻譯成「對不起。」注意這句話不是用在跟對方道歉時,而是用在「你遇到不知道的事情,想請問對方」,例如:你要問路、問時間,你要打電話,想問哪裡有電話可以使用,都是先說一句「Excuse me.」以引起對方的注意,他會注意聽你要說什麼,這時候你再問你要問的問題。

或是對方擋住了你的去路,你想請對方讓路,這時你只要開口說「Excuse me.」,對方如果是個懂英語的人,馬上就知道你是要請他讓路。

會話靈活練習

▶ **問哪裡有電話**

A Excuse me. Do you know where the nearest phone is?
對不起,你知道最近的電話在哪裡嗎?

B There should be one in the library.
圖書館裡應該有一支電話。

▶ **在自助餐廳與不認識的人搭訕**

A Do you eat at this cafeteria often?
你常在這家自助餐廳吃飯嗎?

B No. Only once in a while.
不常，只是偶爾來。

▶ 在美國大使館前

A Excuse me. Is this the American embassy?
對不起，這裡是美國大使館嗎？

B Yes, it is.
是的。

▶ 請問別人，哪裡可以買到地圖

A Good evening.
晚安。

　　Do you know where I could buy a map?
　　你知道哪裡可以買到地圖嗎？

B Try asking at the gas station.
到加油站去問問看。

▶ 問對方會不會說英語

A Excuse me. Do you speak English?
對不起，你會說英語嗎？

B Yes. Can I help you?
會，有什麼事嗎？

英語會話單字

☑ arrive	[əˈraɪv]	抵達
☑ minute	[ˈmɪnɪt]	（時間單位）分
☑ mind	[maɪnd]	v. 介意
☑ food	[fud]	食物
☑ nearest	[ˈnɪrɪst]	最靠近的（near 的最高級）
☑ should	[ʃʊd]	應該
☑ library	[ˈlaɪˌbrɛrɪ]	圖書館
☑ cafeteria	[ˌkæfəˈtɪrɪə]	自助餐廳
☑ embassy	[ˈɛmbəsɪ]	大使館
☑ buy	[baɪ]	買
☑ map	[mæp]	地圖
☑ station	[ˈsteʃən]	站台
☑ gas station		加油站

Unit 4

Where are you moving?
你要搬去哪裡？

MP3-05

對話一

A Are you moving?
你要搬家嗎？

B Yes.
是的。

A Where are you moving?
你要搬去哪裡？

B I'm moving to New York.
我要搬到紐約。

A When do you leave?
你什麼時候走？

B Next week.
下星期。

對話二

A How are you travelling?
你要怎麼走？

B I'm travelling by train.
我要搭火車。

A When are you leaving?
你什麼時候走？

B I leave tomorrow night.
我明天晚上走。

純美語解說

　　本單元裡，A 和 B 兩個人是在談一些「已經計畫好要去做的事」，例如：要搬家、要離開、要搭火車走等等，像這種已經計畫好要做的事，在英語會話中都是要用「現在進行式」，來說這件已經計畫好要去做的事。所謂的現在進行式就是「am、are、is ＋現在分詞」，例如：「我明天要搬家（move）。」這是件已經計畫好的事，要說「I am moving tomorrow.」。

　　以上這種已經計畫好的事，除了用現在進行式外，美國人有時候也會用現在式來說，例如問：「你什麼時候走（leave）？」，英語的問法可以是：「When do you leave?」和「When are you leaving?」兩種，而要回答這句話，可以說「I'm leaving tomorrow.」或「I leave tomorrow.」。

會話靈活練習

▶ 問對方要搬到哪裡

A Where are you moving?
你要搬到哪裡？

B I'm moving to Washington.
我要搬到華盛頓。

▶ 問對方何時要離開

A When do you leave?
你什麼時候走？

B I leave next Friday.
我下星期五走。

▶ 問對方行李都整理好了嗎

A Have you finished packing your things?
你的行李都裝好了嗎？

B Yes. I finished packing yesterday.
是的，我昨天就裝好了。

▶ 對方好像要出遠門

A Are you leaving?
你要出遠門嗎？

B Yes. I'm leaving tomorrow.
是的，我明天走。

▶ 問飛機幾點起飛

A When does your plane leave?
你的飛機幾點起飛？

B My plane leaves in two hours.
我的飛機再兩小時就要起飛。

英語會話單字

☑ train	[tren]	火車；訓練
☑ leave	[liv]	離開
☑ pack	[pæk]	裝箱；打點行李
☑ yesterday	[ˈjɛstɚde]	昨天
☑ tomorrow	[təˈmɑro]	明天
☑ plane	[plen]	飛機
☑ hour	[aʊr]	（時間單位）小時

Unit 5

How do you like the party?
你喜歡這個宴會嗎？

MP3-06

▶ 對話一

A How do you like the party?
你喜歡這個宴會嗎？

B It's great.
這個宴會很棒。

A Would you like a drink?
你要喝飲料嗎？

B Yes. Please.
好的。

A What would you like?
你要喝什麼？

B I would like a coke.
我要可樂。

Thank you.
謝謝你。

▶ 對話二

A Do you know many people here?
這裡的人你認識很多嗎？

B No.
不多。

A Would you like me to introduce you to some people?
你要不要我介紹你認識一些人？

B Yes. I would like that.
好的，那很好。

純美語解說

　　如果要用英語問對方：「你要什麼？」照字面翻譯，好像應該是「What do you want?」；但是千萬要注意，這是一句太直接的話，一般受過教育的美國人很少這麼說，正如作者在其它的英語著作中常提到的，英美人士講話很委婉，所以當你想用英語問對方想要什麼的時候，最好說「What would you like?」。大家學英語時，應該學過「would like」就是「想要」的意思，所以，若你問對方「要喝飲料嗎？」同樣地也是用「would like」這個片語，整句話就是「Would you like a drink?」。

會話靈活練習

▶ **主人歡迎客人來參加宴會**

A Hi. Welcome to the party.
嗨，歡迎來參加宴會。

B Thanks.
謝謝。

▶ 在宴會中與人搭訕

A How did you hear about the party?
你怎麼知道有這個宴會？

B A friend of mine told me.
有個朋友跟我說的。

▶ 在宴會中與人搭訕

A Do you go to parties often?
你常參加宴會嗎？

B I go when I have time.
我有時間才去。

▶ 問對方從哪裡來的

A Where are you from?
你從哪裡來的？

B I'm from Taiwan.
我來自台灣。

▶ 問對方要不要喝什麼飲料

A What would you like to drink?
你要喝什麼飲料？

B I'll take a coke please.
我想喝可樂。

英語會話單字

☑ **party** ['pɑrtɪ] 宴會；派對

☑ **great** [gret] 很好

☑ **drink** [drɪŋk] 飲料

☑ **people** ['pipl̩] 人們

☑ **introduce** [ˌɪntrə'djus] 介紹

☑ **welcome** ['wɛlkəm] 歡迎

☑ **often** ['ɔfən] 時常

MEMO

Chapter 2

朋友間的英語

It's very cold today.
今天真冷。

▶ 對話一

◉ MP3-07

A How do you like the weather?
這種天氣你喜歡嗎？

B It's lovely.
很棒。

A Do you know if it will rain tomorrow?
你知道明天會下雨嗎？

B No. I haven't heard the forecast.
不知道，我沒有聽氣象預報。

▶ 對話二

A It's very cold today.
今天真冷。

B Yes. I heard that it might snow tonight.
是啊，我聽說今晚可能會下雪。

A Will it snow tomorrow?
明天會下雪嗎？

B Probably.
可能會。

Chapter 2

I heard that there is a high chance for snow tomorrow.
我聽說明天下雪的機會很大。

純美語解說

當我們說到天氣時，英語就是用「it」這個字，接著再來看我們要說「天氣怎麼樣」的句型。如果是用形容詞來說天氣，句型就是「It is＋天氣的情況。」例如：出大太陽（sunny），那就是「It is sunny.」；說到很冷（cold），整句話就是「It is cold.」形容天氣的形容詞很多，最常見的有 hot、cold、cool、sunny、cloudy、windy、lovely。

如果我們說的是天氣的動作，例如：下雨（rain）、下雪（snow）、結冰（ice），就是「It」後面接這個天氣的動作，也就是這些動詞。不過大家都知道，英語的動詞要注意時式，例如：「現在在下雨。」要用現在進行式，說法是「It is raining.」；「明天會下雪。」要用未來式，說法是「It will snow tomorrow.」。

會話靈活練習

▶ 問在下雨嗎

A Is it raining outside?
外面在下雨嗎？

B Yes. You might want to bring an umbrella.
是的，你可能要帶把傘。

▶ 說今天真熱

A It's really hot today.
今天真的很熱。

B I agree.
我同意。

　　Let's go inside, where it's cooler.
　　我們到裡頭去，那裡比較涼。

▶ 說今天的天氣

A It snowed a lot today.
今天的雪下得真多。

B Yes. It's supposed to snow the rest of the week.
是啊，接下來整個星期應該都會下雪。

▶ 問明天的天氣會如何

A Do you know the forecast for tomorrow?
你知道明天的氣象預報嗎？

B I heard that it will be clear and sunny.
我聽說明天天氣晴朗，出大太陽。

▶ 問某個地方的氣候如何

A What's the weather like in Washington?
華盛頓的天氣如何？

B It's usually very cloudy.
通常都是陰沈沈的。

　　It rains most of the time.
　　大半的時間是在下雨。

英語會話單字

☑ weather	[ˈwɛðɚ]	天氣
☑ lovely	[ˈlʌvlɪ]	（口語）令人愉快的； 美好的
☑ rain	[ren]	v. 下雨
☑ heard	[hɝd]	聽見（hear 的過去式）
☑ forecast	[ˈforˌkæst]	預測
☑ snow	[sno]	下雪
☑ probably	[ˈprɑbəblɪ]	或許，可能的
☑ chance	[tʃæns]	機會
☑ outside	[ˈaʊtˈsaɪd]	外面
☑ umbrella	[ʌmˈbrɛlə]	雨傘
☑ really	[ˈriəlɪ]	真的
☑ supposed	[səˈpozd]	（口語）應該
☑ rest	[rɛst]	其餘的
☑ clear	[klɪr]	晴朗
☑ sunny	[ˈsʌnɪ]	出大太陽的
☑ usually	[ˈjuʒʊəlɪ]	通常
☑ cloudy	[ˈklaʊdɪ]	多雲的

I saw Mary at school today.

我今天在學校遇到瑪莉。

🔘 MP3-08

▶ 對話一

A Have you seen John lately?
你最近有看到約翰嗎？

B Yes. I saw him yesterday.
有，我昨天看到他。

A How is he doing?
他怎麼樣？

B He's doing great.
他很好。

▶ 對話二

A I saw Mary at school today.
我今天在學校遇到瑪莉。

B Is she in one of your classes?
她有課跟你同一班嗎？

A No. I bumped into her in the hallway.
沒有，我在走道上遇到她的。

B Was she going to class?
她要去上課嗎？

A Yes. She was going to her history class.
是的，她要去上她的歷史課。

會話靈活練習

問某個朋友的狀況

A Is John still working on campus?
約翰還在學校上班嗎？

B Yes. He has his own office now.
是的，他現在有他自己的辦公室。

問某個朋友何時畢業

A When does Mary graduate?
瑪莉什麼時候畢業？

B I think she graduates next semester.
我想她下個學期畢業。

有個朋友在生病

A Is Mary still sick?
瑪莉還在生病嗎？

B No. She's much better now.
沒有，她現在好多了。

▶ 朋友過生日

A Tomorrow is John's birthday.
明天是約翰的生日。

B We should get him a present.
我們應該買個禮物給他。

▶ 問某個朋友做簡報的情形

A How did John's presentation go?
約翰的簡報做得怎麼樣？

B It was a success.
做得很成功。

英語會話單字

☐ lately	['letlɪ]	近來；最近的
☐ bump	[bʌmp]	撞到
☐ hallway	['hɔl,we]	走道
☐ history	['hɪstərɪ]	歷史
☐ campus	['kæmpəs]	校園
☐ office	['ɔfɪs]	辦公室
☐ graduate	['grædʒʊ,et]	畢業
☐ semester	[sə'mɛstɚ]	學期
☐ present	['prɛzn̩t]	禮物
☐ presentation	[,prɛzn̩'teʃən]	簡報
☐ success	[sək'sɛs]	成功

Unit 8

Where are you going for vacation?

你要去哪裡度假？

MP3-09

 對話一

A Where are you going for vacation?
你要去哪裡度假？

B I think I'll go to New York.
我想我會到紐約去。

A Oh? Is it nice there?
哦？紐約是個好地方嗎？

B Yes. It's beautiful.
是，紐約很漂亮。

 對話二

A Where did you take your last vacation?
你上次去哪裡度假？

B I went to Paris.
我去巴黎。

A Did you go to any art museums?
你有沒有去參觀藝術博物館？

B Yes. I went to the Louvre.
有，我去羅浮宮。

當你要告訴對方,「如果我是你(If I were you),我會這麼做(I would...)」,這種說法常把「If I were you」這幾個字省略掉,而直接說「I would 這麼做。」例如: 對方在考慮不知道要去哪裡度假,你就可以跟他說「I would go to Canada.」,這句話含有「是我的話,我會去加拿大」的意思。

會話靈活練習

▶ 問對方什麼時候休假

A When will you take your next vacation?
你下次什麼時候休假?

B Probably at the beginning of next Summer.
可能明年夏天一開始的時候。

▶ 請對方建議度假地點

A Where should I go for my vacation?
我該去哪裡度假?

B I would go to Canada.
我會去加拿大。

It's very pretty there.
那個地方很美。

▶ 問對方要休假多久

A How long is your vacation going to be?
你假期有多久?

B I have three weeks.
我有三個星期的假。

問對方要休假嗎

A Are you thinking of taking a vacation?
你在考慮要休假嗎?

B Yes. I would like to take one soon.
是,我很快就會休假。

請教對方度假地

A Is Austria a good place for a vacation?
奧地利是休假的好地方嗎?

B Yes. There are many beautiful mountains there.
是,那裡有許多漂亮的山。

英語會話單字

☐ **vacation**	[ve'keʃən]	休假;假期
☐ **beautiful**	['bjutəfəl]	美麗的;漂亮的
☐ **last**	[læst]	上一次的
☐ **art**	[ɑrt]	藝術
☐ **next**	[nɛkst]	下一個
☐ **beginning**	[bɪ'ɡınıŋ]	開始
☐ **museum**	[mju'ziəm]	博物館
☐ **mountain**	['maʊntn̩]	山

Unit 9

Did you vote?
你有沒有去投票？

▶ 對話一

MP3-10

A Who do you think you will vote for?
你會投票給誰？

B I don't know.
我不知道。

I'm still learning about the issues.
我還在研究各個候選人提出的議題。

A Do you think you will vote?
你想你會去投票嗎？

B Probably.
可能會。

▶ 對話二

A Did you vote?
你有沒有去投票？

B Yes.
有。

A What party did you vote for?
你投給哪個政黨？

B I voted for the independent party.
我投給無黨派的。

純美語解說

　　當你要問對方，有沒有去投票時，問的是一件過去的動作「去投票（vote）」，所以要注意這句話裡的過去式助動詞「did」。當你要問一件過去的動作時，要說「Did you ＋你要問對方有沒有做的事？」，所以你要問對方有沒有去投票，英語就是「Did you vote?」。

會話靈活練習

▶ 談起某個法案

A Did you hear about the bill that congress passed?
你聽說國會剛通過的法案嗎？

B Yes. The bill was very popular.
聽說了，這個法案很受歡迎。

▶ 談起總統的動向

A The president met with the ambassador of France yesterday.
總統昨天跟法國大使見面。

B Yes. I read about it in the paper.
是，我在報紙上看到這個消息。

▶ 談起選舉

A When are the elections?
選舉在什麼時候？

B At the beginning of next year.
在明年初。

談起政治

A Do you enjoy politics?
你喜歡政治嗎？

B Yes. I think politics is very interesting.
是，我認為政治很有趣。

談起投票

A Do you usually vote?
你通常都有去投票嗎？

B Yes. I almost always vote.
有，我差不多都去投了。

英語會話單字

☐ vote	[vot]	投票
☐ learn	[lɜn]	學習
☐ issue	[ˈɪʃjʊ]	議題；問題
☐ party	[ˈpɑrtɪ]	政黨；黨派
☐ independent	[ˌɪndɪˈpɛndənt]	無黨派的
☐ bill	[bɪl]	法案
☐ congress	[ˈkɑŋgrəs]	國會
☐ pass	[pæs]	通過

☑ **popular** ['pɑpjələ˞] 受歡迎的

☑ **president** ['prɛzədənt] 總統

☑ **ambassador** [æm'bæsədə˞] 大使

☑ **paper** ['pepə˞] 報紙

（newspaper 的簡寫）

☑ **election** [ɪ'lɛkʃən] 選舉

☑ **enjoy** [ɪn'dʒɔɪ] 喜歡；感到樂趣

☑ **politics** ['pɑlə,tɪks] 政治

☑ **interesting** ['ɪntərɪstɪŋ] 有趣的

☑ **almost** ['ɔl,most] 差不多都有

☑ **always** ['ɔlwez] 總是

How many classes are you taking?
你修幾門課？

🔘 MP3-11

▶ 對話一

A Are you taking math this semester?
這學期你有修數學嗎？

B Yes.
有。

A Do you have a good professor?
你們的教授好嗎？

B Yes. He's a very good teacher.
很好，他是一個非常好的老師。

▶ 對話二

A How long is it before you graduate?
你還有多久畢業？

B I graduate in one year.
還有一年。

A Are you going to graduate school?
你要念研究所嗎？

B Yes. I want to get a Master's degree.
要，我要拿碩士學位。

A How long will that take?
要多少年？

B Two years.
兩年。

純美語解說

「take」這個字有很多意思，在學校修課就是用「take」這個動詞，例如：「Last year I took two science classes.」（去年我上了兩門科學課。）「I took six credits my senior year.」（我大四修六學分。）做某件事要花多少時間也是用「take」這個動詞，例如：「How long will it take to get there?」（到那裡要多久？）

會話靈活練習

▶ 談修課

A How many classes are you taking?
你修幾門課？

B I'm taking five classes this semester.
這學期我修五科。

▶ 談期末考

A Are you prepared for final exams?
期末考你準備好了嗎？

B I think so.
準備好了。

➤ 談期中考

A How did you do on your mid-term exam?
你期中考考得如何？

B Excellent. I got an A.
考得很好。我的成績是 A。

➤ 談學校研究作業

A Are you still working on that project?
你還在做研究作業嗎？

B Yes, but I'm almost finished.
是的，但是我快做完了。

➤ 談家庭作業

A Do you have a lot of homework?
你有很多家庭作業嗎？

B Yes. I have a lot.
有，很多。

英語會話單字

☐ math	[mæθ]	數學
☐ semester	[sə'mɛstɚ]	學期
☐ professor	[prə'fɛsɚ]	教授
☐ degree	[dɪ'gri]	學位
☐ prepare	[prɪ'pɛr]	準備

☑ final	[ˈfaɪnl̩]	最後的
☑ exam	[ɪgˈzæm]	考試
		（examination 的縮寫）
☑ mid-term	[ˈmɪdˌtɝm]	期中考
☑ excellent	[ˈɛksələnt]	很棒的
☑ project	[ˈprɑdʒɛkt]	學校研究作業
☑ finish	[ˈfɪnɪʃ]	完成
☑ homework	[ˈhomˌwɝk]	家庭作業

Chapter 2

Unit 11

Do you read often?
你常看書嗎？

▶ 對話一

A Do you read often?
你常看書嗎？

B Yes. I read several books a month.
是，我一個月看好幾本書。

A What do you read?
你都看什麼書？

B I like to read classical literature.
我喜歡看古典文學。

▶ 對話二

A Have you read anything lately?
你最近有看什麼書嗎？

B Yes. I just finished reading Milton's "Paradise Lost".
有，我最近剛看完米爾頓的《失樂園》。

A What did you think of it?
你認為那本書怎麼樣？

B It was very entertaining.
娛樂性很高。

純美語解說

在說英語時，中國人所遇到的問題就是時式不會用，所以外國人常常搞不清楚你到底在說現在的事情，還是過去的事情，還是你正要去做的事情。其實英語的動詞時式有一定的規則，只要瞭解了，問題也就迎刃而解。

當你要說一件沒有時間性的事情，也就是這件事跟時間無關時，要用「現在簡單式」，例如：你想知道對方的生活習慣、嗜好，這跟時間無關，所以你就要用「現在簡單式」來問。又如：你要問對方常看書嗎、他看不看書，這些是一種平常的生活習慣，既不是問他現在是不是正在看書、昨天有沒有看書，也不是問他明天要不要看書，因此，對方看書的習慣與時間無關，所以要用「現在簡單式」，英語的說法就是「Do you read often?」。同樣地，問你去不去書店，也是要用現在簡單式，英語的說法就是「Do you go to bookstores?」。

會話靈活練習

▶ 談看書

A Do you read literature?
你看文學作品嗎？

B Certainly. I have a large library.
當然，我收藏了很多文學作品。

▶ 談作者

A Who's your favorite author?
你最喜歡哪個作者？

B I like Hemingway.
我喜歡海明威。

談看書

A Do you have a favorite book?
有哪一本書是你最喜歡的嗎？

B Yes. I love Mary Shelley's "Frankenstein".
有，我喜歡瑪莉薛力的《科學怪人》。

談書店

A Do you go to bookstores?
你去書店嗎？

B Sometimes.
有時候會去。

談古典名著

A Have you read all of the classics?
你看過所有的古典文學嗎？

B Not yet.
沒有。

There are still many that I have not read.
還有許多我沒有看過。

英語會話單字

☑ **often** ['ɔfən] 時常

☑ **several** ['sɛvərəl] 幾個

☑ **month** [mʌnθ] 月

☑ **classical** ['klæsɪkl̩] 古典的

☑ **literature** ['lɪtərətʃɚ] 文學

☑ **entertaining** [ɛntɚ'tenɪŋ] 有趣的

☑ **library** ['laɪˌbrɛrɪ] 圖書館

☑ **favorite** ['fevərɪt] 最喜歡的

☑ **author** ['ɔθɚ] 作者

☑ **bookstore** ['bʊkˌstor] 書店

☑ **classics** ['klæsɪks] 文學名著；經典作品

MEMO

Chapter 3

社交英語

Unit 12

Would you like to go out for some coffee?
你要不要出去喝杯咖啡？

🔘 MP3-13

▶ 對話一

A Would you like to come to the movies with us Saturday?
你星期六要跟我們一起去看電影嗎？

B What time is the movie showing?
幾點的電影？

A Three o'clock.
三點。

Do you have time?
你有時間嗎？

B Yes. I would like to go.
有，我想去。

Thank you.
謝謝你。

▶ 對話二

A We would like to invite you to dinner tonight.
我們想邀你今晚來吃晚飯。

B That's very kind of you.
你們真好。

🄰 Will you come?
你能來嗎？

🄱 Yes. I would like that very much.
可以，我很高興你們邀請我。

會話靈活練習

▶ 請對方來開會

🄰 You're invited to the meeting tonight.
請來參加今晚的會議。

🄱 Thank you.
謝謝你的邀請。

I'll be there.
我會到。

▶ 邀約

🄰 Would you like to come to the seminar tonight?
你要來參加今晚的講習會嗎？

🄱 Thank you, but I don't have the time.
謝謝你，但是我沒有時間。

▶ 請對方來參加宴會

🄰 You're invited to the party tomorrow.
請來參加明天的宴會。

B Thanks.
謝謝你。

▶ 請對方來參加招待會

A Please come to the reception tonight.
請來參加今晚的招待會。

B Thank you, but I can't.
謝謝你的邀請，但是我不能來。

▶ 邀對方去喝咖啡

A Would you like to go out for some coffee?
你要不要出去喝杯咖啡？

B Yes. That sounds great.
好，這個主意不錯。

英語會話單字

☑ movie	['muvɪ]	電影
☑ showing	['ʃoɪŋ]	上演
☑ o'clock	[ə'klɑk]	（時間）～點鐘
☑ invite	[ɪn'vaɪt]	邀請
☑ kind	[kaɪnd]	a. 良善
☑ meeting	['mitɪŋ]	會議
☑ seminar	['sɛmə͵nɑr]	講習會

☑ **party** ['pɑrtɪ] 宴會;派對

☑ **reception** [rɪ'sɛpʃən] 招待會;歡迎會

☑ **sound** [saʊnd] v. 聽起來

Would you like some tea?
你要喝茶嗎？

🔘 MP3-14

▶ 對話一

A Is this the drama club meeting?
這是戲劇社的會議嗎？

B Yes. Please take a seat.
是的，請坐。

A Thank you.
謝謝你。

When does the meeting begin?
會議什麼時候開始？

B The meeting will start in five minutes.
會議再五分鐘就開始。

▶ 對話二

A Hi. I'm here for the dinner party.
嗨，我是來參加晚宴的。

B Welcome. Please come in.
歡迎，請進。

A Thank you.
謝謝你。

Has anyone else arrived?
有其他的人到了嗎？

B Yes. They're in the dining room.
有，他們在餐廳。

May I take your coat?
要我幫你把外套拿去放嗎？

A Yes. Thank you.
好的，謝謝你。

純美語解說

當你去參加宴會，進到主人家時，主人通常會幫你把你脫下的外套拿去掛好，這時他就會跟你說「May I take your coat?」或「Let me take your coat.」。在這裡，主人說要幫你「take your coat」，意思就是要幫你把外套拿去掛好。

會話靈活練習

▶ 到一個宴會

A Hi. Is this the party?
嗨，這裡就是宴會的地方嗎？

B Yes. Please come in.
是的，請進。

▶ 請客人喝茶

A Would you like some tea?
你要喝茶嗎？

B Yes. Please.
好的，請倒一杯給我。

▶ 參加會議

A Is the meeting starting?
會議開始了嗎？

B Yes.
開始了。

▶ 晚飯後

A The dinner was wonderful.
晚餐很棒。

B Thank you.
謝謝你。

I'm glad you enjoyed it.
我很高興你喜歡今晚的菜。

▶ 主人待客

A How do you like the tea?
這個茶你喜歡嗎？

B It's very good.
很好。

Thank you.
謝謝你。

英語會話單字

☑ drama	[ˈdrɑmə]	戲劇
☑ club	[klʌb]	社團
☑ seat	[sit]	座位
☑ begin	[bɪˈgɪn]	開始
☑ start	[stɑrt]	開始
☑ arrive	[əˈraɪv]	抵達
☑ coat	[kot]	外套
☑ wonderful	[ˈwʌndɚfəl]	好棒的；絕妙的；好極了

MEMO

Chapter 4

飲食英語

Unit 14

May I take your order?
你要點菜了嗎？

▶ 對話一　　　　　　　　　　　　　🔘 MP3-15

A Hello. I'd like to order some French fries.
哈囉，我要點一些炸薯條。

B Would you like anything else with that?
還要其他什麼東西嗎？

A No, that will be all.
不用，這樣就行了。

　Thank you.
　謝謝你。

B Certainly. That will be one dollar please.
好，那要一塊錢。

▶ 對話二

A Hello. May I take your order?
哈囉，你要點菜了嗎？

B Yes, I would like a hamburger.
是，我要一個漢堡。

A Would you like a drink with that?
你要飲料嗎？

B Yes, I'll take a coke.
是，我要可樂。

A Thank you.
謝謝你。

會話靈活練習

▶ 點食物的說法之一

A Hi. May I take your order?
嗨，你要點菜了嗎？

B Yes, I'll take a hamburger please.
可以，我要一個漢堡。

▶ 點食物的說法之二

A Hi. Could I get French fries and a coke?
嗨，我想要炸薯條和可樂。

B Certainly. Anything else?
好的，還要其他什麼東西嗎？

▶ 點食物的說法之三

A Hello. I'd like to order a shake.
哈囉，我要點個奶昔。

B Will that be all?
還要其他什麼東西嗎？

點食物的說法之四

A Can I help you?
你需要什麼？

B Yes, I'll take two hamburgers.
是，我要兩個漢堡。

點食物的說法之五

A What would you like?
你要什麼？

B I'd like a slice of pizza please.
我要一片比薩餅。

英語會話單字

☑ order	[ˈɔrdɚ]	v. 點菜
☑ order	[ˈɔrdɚ]	n. 點菜
☑ dollar	[ˈdɑlɚ]	（貨幣單位）元
☑ hamburger	[ˈhæmˈbɝgɚ]	漢堡；絞牛肉
☑ drink	[drɪŋk]	飲料
☑ certainly	[ˈsɝtṇlɪ]	當然；當然可以
☑ shake	[ʃek]	（飲料）奶昔
☑ slice	[slaɪs]	一片

Unit 15

Would you like to be seated?

我帶你們入座好嗎？

 MP3-16

Chapter 4

 對話一

A Hi. Would you like to be seated?
嗨，我帶你們入座好嗎？

B Yes, please.
好的。

A Would you like a table or a booth?
你們要一般的桌位，還是要沙發座？

B We'll take a booth please.
我們要沙發座。

 對話二

A Good evening.
晚安。

Where would you like to be seated?
你們想要坐哪裡？

B Could we have a table by the window please?
我們可以坐靠窗的桌位嗎？

A Certainly. Right this way.
可以，請往這裡走。

B Thank you.
謝謝你。

A Will this table do?
這張桌子可以嗎?

B Yes, thank you.
可以,謝謝你。

會話靈活練習

▶ 服務生帶客人入座

A May I seat you?
我帶你入座好嗎?

B Yes, please.
好的,謝謝。

▶ 問要抽煙區還是非抽煙區

A Would you like smoking or non-smoking?
你要抽煙區還是非抽煙區?

B We would like non-smoking please.
我們要非抽煙區。

▶ 服務生帶客人入座

A Where would you like to be seated?
你們想要坐哪裡?

B I'll take a booth please.
我們要坐沙發座。

▶ 請服務生帶位

A Hello. May I help you?
哈囉，需要我幫忙嗎？

B Yes, we would like to be seated please.
是，我們等著服務生帶位入座。

▶ 服務生帶客人入座

A Would you like to be seated outside or inside?
你們要坐在室外還是室內？

B We'll sit outside.
我們要坐在室外。

　　Thank you.
謝謝你。

英語會話單字

☑ booth	[buθ]	（餐館中的）沙發座
☑ seat	[sit]	座位；就座
☑ window	['wɪndo]	窗戶
☑ way	[we]	方向
☑ smoking	['smokɪŋ]	抽煙區

Unit 16

Can I get you something to drink?
你要喝什麼嗎？

 MP3-17

▶ 對話一

A Hello. What would you like tonight?
哈囉，你今晚要吃什麼？

B Hi. I'll take the lobster please.
嗨，我要龍蝦。

A Certainly. What would you like to drink?
好的，你要喝什麼？

B Bring me a bottle of Champagne.
我要一瓶香檳。

A I'll have that right out to you.
我馬上送出來給你。

B Thank you.
謝謝你。

▶ 對話二

A Good evening.
晚安。

Can I get you something to drink?
你要喝什麼嗎？

B Yes, I'll take a glass of Merlot.
好，我要一杯摩爾樂紅葡萄酒。

A Very well.
很好。

Would you like an appetizer?
你要飯前小菜嗎？

B Yes, I'll take the peanuts.
好，我要一碟花生。

純美語解說

　　「special」這個字當形容詞，是「特別的」的意思，若是當名詞，是指「某件東西在某段時間內以較便宜的價錢在賣」，這個用法在美國的餐廳內常可看到，例如：牌子上寫著「Today's specials（本日特餐）」，下面列出一些菜名，這些菜就是當日的特價餐。若是該餐廳的作法是，一天只有一樣特價餐，那麼牌子上就會寫著「Today's special」，然後只列出一道菜名。有些餐廳會推出「午餐特餐」，它的英語就是「Lunch Specials」。

　　如果你要點菜，但還沒決定要吃什麼，你也可以問服務生：「Do you have a special tonight?」（你們今晚有沒有什麼特價菜？）如果服務生要告訴你有哪一道菜是特價，他回答的句型就是「We have a special on ＋特價的那一道菜.」。

會話靈活練習

▶ 服務生接受點菜

A What would you like this evening?
你今晚要點什麼？

B I would like a salad please.
我要一個沙拉。

▶ 服務生接受點菜

A Hello. What would you like today?
哈囉，你今天要點什麼？

B I have decided on the shrimp.
我決定要蝦子。

▶ 服務生的服務

A May I help you?
有什麼事嗎？

B Could you bring me a coke please?
請拿一杯可樂給我。

▶ 需要服務生的服務

A Could I get the steak meal please?
請給我牛排餐。

B Certainly.
好的。

▶ 問有什麼特價菜

A Do you have a special tonight?
你們今晚有沒有什麼特價菜？

B Yes, we have a special on fried chicken.
有，我們的炸雞是特價。

英語會話單字

☑ lobster   ['lɑbstɚ]   龍蝦

☑ bottle   ['bɑtḷ]   瓶子

☑ glass   [glæs]   玻璃杯

☑ appetizer   ['æpə,taɪzɚ]   （餐前的）開胃小菜

☑ salad   ['sæləd]   沙拉

☑ decide   [dɪ'saɪd]   決定

☑ shrimp   [ʃrɪmp]   蝦

☑ special   ['spɛʃəl]   特價優待；特餐

Excuse me. Waiter.
對不起，服務生。

▶ 對話一　　　　　　　　　　　　　💿 MP3-18

A Excuse me. Waiter.
對不起，服務生。

B Yes, can I help you?
有什麼事嗎？

A Yes, could I get the check please?
請把帳單給我。

B Certainly. I'll get that to you right away.
好，我馬上拿來給你。

A I appreciate it.
謝謝你。

▶ 對話二

A Excuse me.
對不起。

B Yes?
有什麼事嗎？

A We didn't get silverware.
我們沒有餐具。

B I apologize.
對不起。

I'll get some silverware right away.
我馬上拿餐具來。

A Thank you.
謝謝你。

純美語解說

　　當你想提出要求，要對方為你做某件事情時，可以用「Could we ＋你所提出的要求」這個句型。這句話表面上，有點是在徵求同意的意思，實際上卻是在提出要求，這是一種很客套的說法，卻也是美國話裡最常見的說法，例如：你要服務生拿帳單給你，你就可以說「Could I get the check please?」，你要服務生拿紙巾給你，說法就是「Could we get napkins?」，若你想換個座位，就可以跟服務生說「Could we get a different seat, please?」。

會話靈活練習

▶ 在餐廳，要服務

A Excuse me. Could we get napkins?
對不起，請拿餐巾給我們。

B Certainly.
好的。

▶ 要什麼調味醬

A Which dressing would you like with your salad?
你的沙拉要配什麼調味料？

B I'll take ranch dressing, please.
我要 ranch 調味料。

> * 配沙拉的調味料，英語叫做 dressing，調味料有很多種，ranch 是
>   其中一種調味料的名稱。

▶ 在餐廳，要服務

A Could we get some more water?
請再給我們一些水。

B Yes, I'll bring that right out.
好的，我馬上拿來。

▶ 在餐廳，要服務

A Could we get a different seat, please?
我們可以換個座位嗎？

B Yes, where would you like to sit?
可以，你們要坐哪裡？

英語會話單字

☑ waiter	['wetɚ]	侍者
☑ check	[tʃɛk]	n. 帳單
☑ appreciate	[əˈpriʃɪˌet]	感激
☑ silverware	[ˈsɪlvɚˌwɛr]	銀餐具
☑ apologize	[əˈpɑləˌdʒaɪz]	道歉
☑ napkin	[ˈnæpkɪn]	餐巾；紙巾
☑ dressing	[ˈdrɛsɪŋ]	（沙拉）調味醬
☑ different	[ˈdɪfərənt]	不同的

Chapter 5

日常必用英語

Unit 18

I need to send this letter to New York.
我要寄這封信到紐約。

MP3-19

▶ 對話一

A Hello. Could I get a book of stamps please?
哈囉，我要買一本郵票。

B Yes, how many would you like?
好的，幾張一本的？

A Could I get a book of twenty stamps?
請給我二十張一本的好嗎？

B Certainly. That will be six dollars and forty cents please.
好，是六塊錢四十分。

▶ 對話二

A Hi. I would like to send a package first class.
嗨，我要用第一類郵件寄一個郵包。

B Where would you like to send it?
你要寄去哪裡？

A I'm sending it to New York.
我要寄到紐約。

B All right.
好。

純美語解說

郵寄郵件通常可分為幾類郵件，用第一類郵件寄比較快，但比較貴。通常比較重且沒什麼時間緊迫性的郵件，有時會用第四類郵件寄，雖然比較慢，但是比較便宜。第一類郵件的英語就是「first class mail」，第四類郵件的英語是「fourth class mail」。

會話靈活練習

▶ 寄易碎物品

A I would like to send something fragile.
我要寄一些易碎的物品。

B That will cost extra.
那郵費會貴一點。

▶ 空運郵件

A I would like to send something by airmail.
我要用空運寄東西。

B How large is the package?
郵件有多大？

▶ 問郵資

A How much is the postage for this letter?
這封信的郵資是多少？

B That would be thirty-two cents.
是三十二分錢。

▶ 購買郵票

A I'd like to purchase a book of five-cent stamps, please.
我要買一本每張是五分錢的郵票。

B Sure. One moment please.
好的，稍等。

▶ 到郵局拿郵件

A I'm here to pick up a package.
我來拿郵件。

B What's your name?
你叫什麼名字？

英語會話單字

☐ stamp	[stæmp]	郵票
☐ send	[sɛnd]	寄
☐ package	[ˈpækɪdʒ]	包裹
☐ fragile	[ˈfrædʒəl]	易碎
☐ cost	[kɔst]	v. 花費；成本
☐ extra	[ˈɛkstrə]	額外的；多餘的
☐ airmail	[ˈɛrˌmel]	航空郵件
☐ postage	[ˈpostɪdʒ]	郵資
☐ letter	[ˈlɛtɚ]	信
☐ purchase	[ˈpɝtʃəs]	購買

Unit 19

I would like to open an account.

我要開一個帳戶。

 MP3-20

Chapter 5

▶ 對話一

A Good afternoon.
午安。

Can I help you?
有什麼事嗎？

B Hi. I would like to open an account.
嗨，我要開一個帳戶。

A Certainly. Would you like checking or savings?
好，你要支票帳戶還是儲蓄帳戶？

B I would like both please.
我兩樣都要。

▶ 對話二

A Hi. What can I do for you?
嗨，我能幫你什麼嗎？

B I would like to cash a check.
我有一張支票要兌換現金。

A Certainly. Is this a personal or a business check?
好的，是私人支票還是公司支票？

B This is a business check.
是一張公司支票。

到銀行，要查存款額

A Hello. May I help you?
哈囉，有什麼事嗎？

B Yes, I would like to check my balance.
是，我要查我的存款額。

到銀行，要提款

A Could I make a withdrawal please?
我要提款。

B Yes, how much would you like to withdraw?
好，你要提多少？

到銀行，要申請貸款

A Hello. Can I help you today?
哈囉，有什麼事嗎？

B Yes, I would like to apply for a loan.
有，我要申請貸款。

到銀行，要存款

A Hi. I would like to make a deposit of five hundred dollars.
嗨，我要存款五百元。

B You will need to fill out a deposit slip please.
你需要填存款單。

到銀行，要申請自動提款卡

A Hi. Could I apply for an ATM card?
嗨，我想申請自動提款卡。

B Sure. Please fill out this application.
好，請填這張申請表。

英語會話單字

☐ account	[əˈkaʊnt]	帳戶
☐ savings	[ˈsevɪŋz]	儲蓄
☐ both	[boθ]	兩者都
☐ cash	[kæʃ]	v. 兌換現金
☐ personal	[ˈpɝsənl̩]	私人的
☐ business	[ˈbɪznɪs]	商務
☐ check	[tʃɛk]	v. 查閱；查一查
☐ check	[tʃɛk]	n. 支票
☐ balance	[ˈbæləns]	存款額
☐ withdrawal	[wɪðˈdrɔəl]	n. 提款

☐ withdraw	[wɪð'drɔ]	v. 提款
☐ apply	[ə'plaɪ]	v. 申請
☐ loan	[lon]	貸款
☐ deposit	[dɪ'pɑzɪt]	存款
☐ slip	[slɪp]	n. 紙條
☐ application	[ˌæplə'keʃən]	n. 申請表
☐ fill out		填寫
☐ apply for		申請

Unit
20
Do you accept checks?
你們收支票嗎？

 對話一 MP3-21

A Excuse me. Could you tell me where the coffee is?
對不起，請你告訴我咖啡放在哪裡。

B The coffee is on aisle three.
咖啡放在第三排。

A Thank you.
謝謝你。

B You're welcome.
不用客氣。

對話二

A Hello. How are you today?
哈囉，你好嗎？

B I'm fine.
很好。

A Do you accept checks?
你們收支票嗎？

B Yes, we do.
我們收。

Chapter 5

當你要付錢時，不管你是想用支票付帳，或是用信用卡付帳，有時你會先問一下店員，他們收不收支票或是信用卡。用英語問對方收不收支票或信用卡，可以用「accept」或「take」這兩個動詞，整句話的說法就是「Do you take checks?」或「Do you accept checks?」或是「Do you take credit cards?」或「Do you accept credit cards?」。

會話靈活練習

▶ 結帳時，店員問客人

A Will that be all today?
你今天就是要買這些嗎？

B Yes, that's everything.
是，就是這些。

▶ 顧客想用支票付款

A Do you take checks at this register?
這個結帳櫃檯收支票嗎？

B No, you'll have to go to the next register.
不收，你必須到下一個結帳櫃檯。

▶ 顧客有折價券

A I would like to use these coupons, please.
我要使用這些折價券。

B I'm sorry.
對不起。

Those coupons have expired.
那些折價券過期了。

▶ 顧客想用信用卡付錢

A Do you take credit cards?
你們收信用卡嗎？

B Yes, of course.
是，我們收。

英語會話單字

☑ coffee	['kɔfɪ]	咖啡
☑ aisle	[aɪl]	（貨架的）行列
☑ accept	[ək'sɛpt]	接受
☑ check	[tʃɛk]	n. 支票
☑ register	['rɛdʒɪstɚ]	收銀機
☑ coupon	['kupɑn]	折價券
☑ expire	[ɪk'spaɪr]	屆期；滿期

I would like to get a haircut.

我想要剪頭髮。

MP3-22

▶ 對話一

A Hi. I would like to get a haircut.
嗨，我想要剪頭髮。

B All right. There will be a fifteen minute wait.
好的，需要等十五分鐘。

A That's fine.
沒關係。

B What's your name?
你叫什麼名字？

A John.
約翰。

▶ 對話二

A How much is a haircut?
剪一次頭髮多少錢？

B Do you want a shampoo also?
你也要洗頭嗎？

A Yes.
要。

B That would be eight dollars.
那要八塊錢。

A All right.
好。

How long is the wait?
要等多久？

B We can take you now.
現在就可以幫你剪。

純美語解說

「shampoo」這個字的意思是「洗髮精」，也可以當「洗頭髮」的意思，當你到美容院，美容師問你要不要洗頭髮，英語的說法就是「Would you like a shampoo?」。

會話靈活練習

▶ 美容師想知道顧客要剪什麼樣子

A How would you like your hair cut?
你的頭髮要剪什麼樣子？

B I would like my hair cut fairly short.
我要剪得很短。

▶ 美容師想知道顧客要不要洗頭

A Would you like a shampoo?
你要不要洗頭？

B Yes, please.
好的。

▶ 剪完頭髮後，美容師問顧客的意見

A How do you like it?
你喜不喜歡？

B It's nice, but could you cut it a little shorter?
很好，但是可不可以剪短一點？

▶ 美容師想知道顧客要不要吹乾

A Do you want me to blow-dry your hair?
你要我幫你把頭髮吹乾嗎？

B Yes, that would be nice.
好，吹乾好。

英語會話單字

☑ haircut	['hɛr‚kʌt]	剪頭髮
☑ wait	[wet]	等
☑ shampoo	[ʃæm'pu]	洗頭
☑ fairly	['fɛrlɪ]	相當
☑ short	[ʃɔrt]	短的
☑ blow-dry	['blo‚draɪ]	吹乾
☑ hair	[hɛr]	頭髮

Unit 22

I'd like to apply for a library card.
我想要申請圖書館借書證。

 MP3-23

▶ 對話一

A Hello. Is this the information desk?
哈囉，這裡是詢問台嗎？

B Yes, it is.
是的。

A I'd like to apply for a library card.
我想要申請圖書館借書證。

B Of course.
好。

You'll need to fill out this form.
你需要填這張表格。

▶ 對話二

A Excuse me. Could you tell me where to find government documents?
對不起，請你告訴我，在哪裡可以找到政府文件。

B Yes, you will find them on the third floor.
好的，你在三樓找得到。

A Thank you very much.
謝謝你。

Chapter 5

B You're welcome.
不客氣。

　到圖書館要把書借出去，英語的說法是要「check out 這些書」，或「check 這些書 out」。「check out」這個片語的意思就是「請圖書館員登記那幾本你要借的書，你就可以借出去」。

會話靈活練習

▶ **要從圖書館借書**

A Hi. I would like to check these books out.
嗨，我要借這些書。

B Very well, do you have your library card?
很好，你有圖書館借書證嗎？

▶ **繳過期書的罰款**

A Hello. I would like to pay the fine on an overdue book.
哈囉，我要付一本過期書的罰款。

B All right, I'll need to see your library card.
好，我需要看你的圖書館借書證。

▶ 問書何時到期

A When will this book be due?
這本書何時到期？

B That will be due as of the fifteenth of November.
十一月十五號到期。

英語會話單字

☑ information	[ˌɪnfɚˈmeʃən]	資料
☑ card	[kɑrd]	會員證
☑ form	[fɔrm]	表格
☑ find	[faɪnd]	找到
☑ government	[ˈgʌvɚnmənt]	政府
☑ document	[ˈdɑkjəmənt]	文件
☑ floor	[flor]	樓層
☑ pay	[pe]	付錢
☑ fine	[faɪn]	罰款
☑ overdue	[ˈovɚˈdu]	過了期
☑ due	[du]	到期；期限截止

MEMO

Chapter 6

選舉英語

Unit 23

What day is the election?
投票是哪一天？

對話一 MP3-24

A Are you registered to vote?
你已經登記要去投票了嗎？

B No, where can I register?
沒有，我要去哪裡登記？

A You can register with the Department of Public Safety.
你可以到監理站去登記。

B I think I'll do that.
我想我會去。

對話二

A Do you know who's running in the next election?
你知道下一次選舉誰要競選嗎？

B No, I don't.
我不知道。

A I'll have to buy a newspaper.
我得去買份報紙。

B You could also watch the news tonight.
你也可以看今晚的新聞。

A Yes, that's a good idea.
是，那是個好主意。

純美語解說

　　Democrat 和 Republican 是美國兩個最大的政黨，「democrat」這個字的意思是「民主」，所以我們叫 Democrat 為「民主黨」，「republican」這個字的意思是「共和」，所以我們叫 Republican 為「共和黨」。

會話靈活練習

問是哪一個政黨

A Are you a member of a political party?
你有沒有參加哪個政黨？

B Yes, I'm a Democrat.
有，我是民主黨。

問要去哪裡投票

A Where do I go to vote?
投票所在哪裡？

B I don't know, but you can call City Hall to find out.
我不知道，但是你可以打電話到市政府去問。

問投票日期

A When are the next elections?
下一次選舉在什麼時候？

B I think they're in November.
我想是在十一月。

問屬於哪個政黨

A Are you Democrat or Republican?
你是民主黨還是共和黨？

B I'm Republican.
我是共和黨。

問投票日期

A What day is the election?
投票是哪一天？

B It's November 15th.
是十一月十五號。

英語會話單字

☑ register	[ˈrɛdʒɪstɚ]	登記
☑ run	[rʌn]	競選
☑ election	[ɪˈlɛkʃən]	選舉
☑ news	[njuz]	新聞
☑ political	[pəˈlɪtɪkl̩]	政治的
☑ Democrat	[ˈdɛməˌkræt]	民主黨
☑ Republican	[rɪˈpʌblɪkən]	共和黨

Who are you voting for?
你要投票給誰？

 對話一 MP3-25

A Which candidate are you voting for?
你要投給哪一個候選人？

B I'm voting for the independent candidate.
我要投給無黨派的候選人。

A Who's ahead in the polls?
誰在民意測驗中領先？

B The Democratic candidate is ahead, but not by much.
民主黨的候選人領先，但是領先不多。

對話二

A Do you consider yourself a Democrat or a Republican?
你自認為是民主黨員還是共和黨員？

B I'm having difficulty deciding.
我沒辦法決定。

A So, which candidate are you going to vote for?
那，你要投票給哪一個候選人？

Chapter 6

B I'll probably vote for the candidate that supports education.
我可能會投給支持教育的候選人。

純美語解說

無黨派的候選人，英語就是「independent candidate」，「independent」的意思是「獨立的」，如果一個候選人不屬於任何一個政黨，那就是一個獨立的候選人。

會話靈活練習

▶ **問支持哪一個候選人**

A Which candidate are you supporting?
你支持哪一個候選人？

B It's difficult for me to decide.
我很難做決定。

They're all supporting similar issues.
他們支持的議題都很相似。

▶ **談候選人**

A The independent candidate is drawing a lot of support.
那個無黨派的候選人吸引很多支持者。

B Yes, he's quite popular.
是，他蠻受歡迎的。

▶ 談民意測驗

A Who's highest in the polls?
誰在民意測驗中領先？

B I think the Republican candidate is.
我想是共和黨的候選人。

▶ 問誰會當選

A Do you think the Democratic candidate will be elected?
你認為民主黨的候選人會選得上嗎？

B It's difficult to say.
很難說。

The candidates are nearly even in the polls.
兩黨候選人在民意測驗中旗鼓相當。

英語會話單字

☑ candidate	[ˈkændəˌdet]	候選人
☑ independent	[ˌɪndɪˈpɛndənt]	無黨派的
☑ ahead	[əˈhɛd]	領先
☑ poll	[pol]	民意測驗
☑ democratic	[ˌdɛməˈkrætɪk]	民主的
☑ consider	[kənˈsɪdɚ]	考慮
☑ support	[səˈport]	支持

Chapter 6

☑ education	[ˌɛdʒəˈkeʃən]	教育
☑ similar	[ˈsɪmələ˞]	相似的
☑ issue	[ˈɪʃjʊ]	問題；議題
☑ draw	[drɔ]	吸引
☑ popular	[ˈpɑpjələ˞]	受歡迎的
☑ elect	[ɪˈlɛkt]	選舉
☑ even	[ˈivən]	相等的

Unit 25 Who is running for Mayor?
誰在競選市長？

MP3-26

 對話一

A Which issue is the Republican candidate supporting?
共和黨的候選人支持哪一個議題？

B He wants to lower the deficit.
他想要降低赤字。

A What is the Democratic candidate supporting?
民主黨的候選人支持哪一個議題？

B He wants to increase educational funding.
他想要增加教育補助經費。

對話二

A Which issues are you supporting?
你支持哪一個議題？

B I'm not sure yet.
我還不太確定。

A There's a campaign rally tonight.
今晚有個競選聯誼會。

Would you like to come?
你要不要來？

Chapter 6

B Sure.
好的。

「run」當「競選」的意思時，常與「for」和「against」這兩個介係詞連用，「run for」是「競選某個職位」的意思，例如：run for President（競選總統）、run for PTA president（競選家長會會長）、run for mayor（競選市長）。

「run against」是「與某人競選」的意思，例如：run against John（與約翰競選）。若是說與某人競選某個職位，說法就是「run against 某人 for 某個職位」，例如：run against John for President（與約翰競選總統）。

▶ 談選舉

A Are you going to vote for the incumbent?
你要投票給現任的候選人嗎？

B No. I would prefer to vote for someone new.
不，我寧願投票給新人。

▶ 談辯論會

A Are you going to watch the debate tonight?
你要看今晚的辯論嗎？

B Yes, I am.
是，我會看。

▶ 談辯論會

A What did you think of the debate?
你認為辯論如何？

B I thought it was very interesting.
我認為很有趣。

▶ 談選舉

A Have you heard anything about the election?
你有沒有聽說選舉任何的事情？

B No, but there will be a special on the news tonight about the election.
沒有，但是今晚會有關於選舉的特別報導。

▶ 記者訪談

A Did you see the interview with the Democratic candidate yesterday?
你有沒有看昨天記者訪談民主黨的候選人？

B Yes, I did.
有，我看了。

英語會話單字

☐ lower	['loɚ]	降低
☐ deficit	['dɛfəsɪt]	赤字；逆差
☐ increase	[ɪn'kris]	增加

☐ educational	[ˌɛdʒəˈkeʃənl]	教育的
☐ funding	[fʌndɪŋ]	贊助
☐ campaign	[kæmˈpen]	競選活動
☐ rally	[ˈrælɪ]	聯誼會；群眾大會
☐ incumbent	[ɪnˈkʌmbənt]	現任的；在職的
☐ prefer	[prɪˈfɝ]	較喜歡
☐ debate	[dɪˈbet]	辯論
☐ special	[ˈspɛʃəl]	（電視的）特別節目
☐ interview	[ˈɪntɚvju]	n. 與記者訪談

Unit 26

Who won the election?
誰當選了？

 對話一

 MP3-27

A The election is being held tomorrow.
明天就要投票了。

B Yes, I'm very excited.
是啊，我蠻興奮的。

A The candidates are neck and neck.
候選人現在是平分秋色。

B It will be a very close election.
明天的選舉結果，肯定會很接近的。

 對話二

A Have all the votes come in?
所有的投票結果都出來了嗎？

B Yes, but they're doing a recount.
出來了，但是他們正在重新計票。

A Who won?
誰當選了？

B They haven't said yet.
他們還沒有說。

Chapter 6

你看過賽馬嗎？在英國的皇家文化裡，賽馬是一種身份的象徵，稍具社會地位的人都以看賽馬為社交生活的一部份，於是在日常生活中，引申自賽馬的英語很多，就像中國人愛看戲，於是有了「粉墨登場」、「下不了台」……等等以戲為喻的日常用語。

「neck and neck」就是來自賽馬的一個喻語。「neck」的原意是「頸子」，當兩匹馬競爭得很厲害時，馬頸應當是平行的，所以說是「頸子對頸子」。在日常生活中，凡是競賽激烈的場合，如選舉、比賽等等，都可以說是「neck and neck」，也就是在「勝負未分」的情況，「鹿死誰手，猶未可知」的意思。

▶ 問選舉結果

A Who won the election?
誰當選了？

B I don't know.
我不知道。

Let's turn on the news.
我們打開新聞來看。

▶ 重新計票

A Did they recount the votes?
他們要重新計票嗎？

B Yes, it was very close.
是的，得票數很接近。

▶ 問有沒有去投票

A Did you vote?
你有沒有去投票？

B Yes, I voted at the last minute.
有，我在最後一分鐘去投的。

▶ 問投票人數

A Did many people vote this election?
這次選舉很多人去投票嗎？

B Yes, a large percentage voted.
是，投票率很高。

▶ 問投票的項目

A Are the congressional elections also being decided?
國會選舉也一起舉行嗎？

B No, those are held two years after the presidential elections.
不，國會選舉是在總統大選之後兩年才舉行。

☐ **held** [hɛld] 舉行（hold 的過去分詞）

☐ **excited** [ɪkˈsaɪtɪd] 感到興奮的

☐ **close** [klos] a. 接近的

☐ **recount** [ˌriˈkaʊnt] 重新計算

☐ **percentage** [pɚˈsɛntɪdʒ] 百分比；百分率

☐ **congressional** [kənˈgrɛʃənl̩] 國會的

☐ **presidential** [ˌprɛzəˈdɛnʃəl] 總統的

Chapter 7

休閒娛樂英語

Unit 27

Would you like to go see a movie?
你要去看電影嗎？

MP3-28

對話一

A Would you like to go see a movie?
你要去看電影嗎？

B Sure, do you know what's playing?
好，你知道在上演什麼嗎？

A No, I'll look in the newspaper.
不知道，我來看看報紙。

B Great!
好。

對話二

A Would you like to see a movie on Saturday?
你星期六要去看場電影嗎？

B Maybe.
也許可以。

What time do you want to go?
你幾點要去？

A I would like to go to the two o'clock showing.
我要去看兩點那一場。

B All right, that sounds good.
好，聽起來不錯。

純美語解說

當有人邀你去看電影，或是你們在約時間，對方說了一個時間，你同意那個時間，你可以隨口回答「That sounds good.」。聽到這句話，你的美國朋友一定覺得你的英語夠溜。注意：「That sounds good. 」「That sounds great.」「That sounds like a great idea.」這些話就是在這種場合用的，簡單一點的說法就是省略掉「that」，說法就是「Sounds good.」「Sounds great.」「Sounds like a good idea.」；當然還有更輕鬆的說法，那就是回答說「Cool ！」，這些都是表示同意。

會話靈活練習

▶ 問電影放映時間

A What time is the movie playing?
電影什麼時候放映？

B It will be showing at seven o'clock.
七點。

▶ 邀約去看電影

A Do you want to go to a movie?
你要去看電影嗎？

B No, thank you.
不，謝謝你。

I'm busy.
我沒時間。

▶ 問有什麼電影在演

A Could you tell me what's playing?
請告訴我有哪些片子在上演。

B Certainly.
好。

▶ 買票看電影

A I would like two tickets to see "Star Wars".
我要兩張「星際大戰」的票。

B That will be ten dollars.
是十塊錢。

▶ 商量要坐哪裡

A Would you like to sit near the screen?
你要坐在靠近銀幕嗎？

B Yes, let's take the first row.
是，我們去坐第一排。

英語會話單字

☑ newspaper	[ˈnjuzˌpepɚ]	報紙
☑ showing	[ˈʃoɪŋ]	上演
☑ show	[ʃo]	（電影）放映
☑ busy	[ˈbɪzɪ]	忙的
☑ ticket	[ˈtɪkɪt]	票
☑ near	[nɪr]	靠近
☑ screen	[skrin]	（電影）銀幕
☑ row	[ro]	排

Unit 28

Would you like to watch the TV?
你要看電視嗎？

MP3-29

對話一

A Would you like to watch the TV?
你要看電視嗎？

B Sure, is there a game playing?
好，有球賽嗎？

A I think there's a soccer game on channel 5.
我想第五頻道有足球賽。

B Let's watch that.
我們來看。

A All right.
好。

對話二

A Do you know which channel the game is on?
你知道球賽在哪一個頻道嗎？

B Yes, it's on channel 10.
知道，在第十頻道。

A Would you like to watch that?
你要看嗎？

B Sure.
好。

會話靈活練習

▶ 談電視節目

A Do you know what's on TV?
你知道電視上在演什麼嗎？

B Yes, there are several good movies on TV right now.
知道，現在有幾部好的電影正在電視上放映。

▶ 電視週刊

A Do you have a TV guide?
你有電視週刊嗎？

B Yes, it's on the counter.
有，在櫃檯上。

▶ 看電視

A Could you turn the TV down?
你可以把電視關小聲一點嗎？

B Sure.
好的。

Chapter 7

▶ 談電視節目

A This is a good show.
這是個好節目。

B Yes, it's very funny.
是的，這個節目很有趣。

▶ 看棒球賽

A Is the baseball game on right now?
現在有棒球賽嗎？

B Yes, it's just starting.
有，剛開始。

英語會話單字

☑ game	[gem]	（球類）比賽
☑ soccer	['sɑkɚ]	足球
☑ channel	['tʃænl̩]	頻道
☑ guide	[gaɪd]	指南
☑ counter	['kaʊntɚ]	櫃檯
☑ show	[ʃo]	節目
☑ funny	['fʌnɪ]	滑稽；有趣的
☑ baseball	['bes,bɔl]	棒球

Unit 29
Which station do you listen to?
你聽哪一個電台？

 MP3-30

 對話一

A Do you mind if I listen to the radio?
我聽收音機你介意嗎？

B No, I don't mind.
不，我不介意。

A Which station do you listen to?
你聽哪一個電台？

B I usually listen to the classical station.
我通常都聽古典電台。

 對話二

A What are you listening to?
你在聽什麼？

B I'm listening to the Beatles.
我在聽披頭四的歌。

A Which song is this?
這是哪一首歌？

B This is "Yesterday".
是「昨天」。

A It's very nice.
很好聽。

▶ 聽收音機

A Could you turn the radio on please?
請把收音機打開。

B All right.
好的。

▶ 聽歌

A Do you like this song?
你喜歡這首歌嗎？

B Yes, this is one of my favorite songs.
是，這是我最喜歡的歌之一。

▶ 聽收音機

A Could you change the station please?
你可以換個電台嗎？

B Sure, what would you like to listen to?
好，你要聽什麼？

聽收音機

A Could you turn the volume down some?
你可以把音量調小聲一點嗎？

B Sure.
好。

聽收音機

A Is this too loud?
這樣會太大聲嗎？

B No, that's fine.
不會，那樣正好。

英語會話單字

☐ mind   [maɪnd]   v. 介意
☐ listen   [ˈlɪsn̩]   聽
☐ station   [ˈsteʃən]   站台
☐ classical   [ˈklæsɪkl̩]   古典的
☐ song   [sɔŋ]   歌
☐ favorite   [ˈfevərɪt]   最喜歡的
☐ change   [tʃendʒ]   改變
☐ volume   [ˈvɑljəm]   音量
☐ loud   [laʊd]   大聲

Chapter 7

Unit 30

Let's rent a movie.
我們去租部電影。

MP3-31

A Would you like to rent a video?
你要去租個錄影帶嗎？

B Yes, that would be great.
好，那很好。

A Do you like comedy?
你喜歡喜劇嗎？

B Yes, I do.
我喜歡。

對話二

A Let's rent a movie.
我們去租部電影。

B All right, what would you like to rent?
好的，你想要租什麼？

A I'd like to rent "Titanic".
我想要租「鐵達尼號」。

B All right, while we're there, let's get "Star Wars", too.
好，我們到了之後，也順便租「星際大戰」。

(會話靈活練習)

▶ 在錄影帶店，要租影片

A Do you have your membership card?
你有會員卡嗎？

B Yes, here you go.
有，在這裡。

▶ 在錄影帶店，要租影片

A I'd like to rent these two videos, please.
我要租這兩支錄影帶。

B All right, can I see your card?
好，請給我看你的會員卡。

▶ 問何時到期

A When are these videos due back?
這些錄影帶什麼時候到期？

B Those will be due tomorrow night.
明天晚上到期。

▶ 要歸還錄影帶

A I would like to return these videos.
我要歸還這些錄影帶。

B Certainly, just lay them on the counter.
好，把它們放在櫃檯上就好。

Chapter 7

▶ 要申請會員證

A Hi. I'd like to apply for a membership card.
嗨，我想要申請會員證。

B Certainly, just fill out this application.
好，把這張申請表填一填。

英語會話單字

☑ rent	[rɛnt]	租借
☑ video	['vɪdɪˌo]	錄影帶
☑ comedy	['kamədɪ]	喜劇
☑ membership	['mɛmbɚˌʃɪp]	會員
☑ due	[du]	到期；期限截止
☑ back	[bæk]	回來
☑ return	[rɪ'tɝn]	歸還
☑ lay	[le]	放置
☑ application	[ˌæplə'keʃən]	n. 申請表

128

Chapter 8

運動英語

What's the score?
比數是多少？

▶ 對話一　　　　　　　　　　　　　　　　　　⊙ MP3-32

A Did you see the baseball game today?
你有看今天的棒球賽嗎？

B Yes.
有。

A Who won?
哪一隊贏？

B Chicago won.
芝加哥隊贏。

A What was the final score?
最後比數是多少？

B Forty one to thirty six.
四十一比三十六。

▶ 對話二

A Do you know who's playing today?
你知道今天的球賽是哪一隊在打嗎？

B Yes, New York versus Boston.
知道，紐約隊對波士頓隊。

A Who do you think will win?
你認為哪一隊會贏？

B I think Boston will win.
我認為波士頓隊會贏。

會話靈活練習

▶ 問球賽的比數

A What's the score?
比數是多少？

B Twenty to ten.
二十比十。

▶ 問哪一隊在打

A Which teams are playing?
哪兩個隊在打？

B San Francisco and Seattle.
三藩市隊和西雅圖隊。

▶ 問球賽的時間

A When is the game?
球賽是什麼時候？

B The game starts in half an hour.
再半個鐘頭開始。

▶ 觀看球賽時

A Which team has the ball?
球在哪一隊手上？

B Seattle has the ball.
在西雅圖隊。

▶ 觀看球賽時

A Do you think Seattle will win?
你認為西雅圖隊會贏嗎？

B No, I think San Francisco will win.
不會，我認為三藩市隊會贏。

英語會話單字

☑ won	[wʌn]	贏（win 的過去式）
☑ final	['faɪn!]	最後的
☑ score	[skor]	分數；得分
☑ versus	['vɝsəs]	（某一隊）對（另一隊）
☑ win	[wɪn]	贏
☑ team	[tim]	隊伍；團隊

Unit 32
Do you like soccer?
你喜歡足球嗎？

 對話一　　　　　　　　　　　🔘 MP3-33

A Do you like soccer?
你喜歡足球嗎？

B Yes, I do.
是，我喜歡足球。

A Would you like to play a game on Saturday?
星期六你要來踢足球嗎？

B Yes, I'd like that.
好的，我喜歡。

How many people will be playing?
多少人會來踢？

A There will be six other people playing.
另外還有六個人。

對話二

A What's your favorite soccer team?
你最喜歡哪個足球隊？

B I like Austria.
我喜歡奧地利隊。

A Really? That's a good team.
真的，那是個好球隊。

Chapter 8

133

B Yes, I hope they win this year.
是的，我希望他們今年會贏。

▶ 邀約踢足球

A Would you like to play some soccer with us?
你要不要跟我們一起踢足球？

B Sure, that sounds like fun.
好，聽起來蠻有趣的。

▶ 答應帶個足球來

A Do you have a soccer ball?
你有足球嗎？

B Yes, I'll bring it.
有，我會帶來。

▶ 找足球場

A Do you know where to find a good soccer field?
你知道該到哪裡找好的足球場嗎？

B Yes, there's a good field next to campus.
知道，學校旁邊有個好的足球場。

▶ 問踢了幾年的足球

A How long have you been playing soccer?
你踢足球踢幾年了？

B I've been playing soccer for five years.
我踢足球踢五年了。

▶ 教如何踢球

A Could you teach me how to play?
你可以教我怎麼踢嗎？

B Certainly.
沒問題。

英語會話單字

☑ soccer	[ˈsɑkɚ]	足球
☑ people	[ˈpipl̩]	人們
☑ fun	[fʌn]	好玩；樂趣
☑ field	[fild]	場地
☑ campus	[ˈkæmpəs]	校園

Chapter 8

Do you exercise?
你運動嗎？

▶ 對話一　　　　　　　　　　　　　　　🔘 MP3-34

A Do you swim?
你游泳嗎？

B Sometimes.
有時候。

A Would you like to come swimming with us?
你要不要跟我們去游泳？

B Sure.
好。

▶ 對話二

A Do you exercise?
你運動嗎？

B Yes, I go running.
是，我跑步。

A How many laps can you run?
你可以跑幾圈？

B I can usually run twenty five laps.
我通常可以跑二十五圈。

這個單元用到了我們在第 11 單元教過的時式用法。如果你想知道對方在運動方面的喜好，我們在第 11 單元說過，當你要說一件沒有時間性的事情時，要用「現在簡單式」，而對方在運動方面的喜好，就是一件跟時間無關的事，所以你要問對方游泳嗎，英語的說法就是「Do you swim?」，你想問對方喜歡跑步嗎，英語的說法就是「Do you like to run?」，都是用「現在簡單式」就行。

談跑步

A Do you like to run?
你喜歡跑步嗎？

B Yes, I love running.
是，我喜歡跑步。

問有沒有跑道

A Is there a track nearby?
附近有跑道嗎？

B Yes, there's a track in the recreational center.
有，休閒中心有個跑道。

邀約去慢跑

A Would you like to go jogging?
你要去慢跑嗎？

B Sure, let me get my jogging shoes.
好，我去拿慢跑鞋。

▶ 談游泳

A Do you swim very often?
你常游泳嗎？

B Yes, I swim three times a week.
是，我一個星期游三次。

▶ 邀約去游泳

A Let's go swimming.
我們去游泳。

B All right, I'll get my swimming suit.
好，我去拿泳衣。

英語會話單字

☑ swim	[swɪm]	游泳
☑ sometimes	['sʌm,taɪmz]	有時
☑ exercise	['ɛksɚ,saɪz]	運動
☑ lap	[læp]	（跑道的）一圈
☑ track	[træk]	跑道
☑ nearby	[nɪr'baɪ]	附近
☑ jogging	['dʒɑgɪŋ]	慢跑

☑ recreational	[͵rɛkrɪˈeʃən!]	娛樂的；休閒的
☑ center	[ˈsɛntɚ]	中心
☑ shoe	[ʃu]	鞋
☑ suit	[sut]	一套衣服

Unit 34

What's your favorite sport?
你最喜歡什麼運動？

MP3-35

▶ 對話一

A What's your favorite sport?
你最喜歡什麼運動？

B I like basketball.
我喜歡籃球。

A Do you know how to play?
你知道怎麼打嗎？

B Yes.
知道。

A Would you like to play a game of one-on-one with me?
你要不要跟我玩一對一的比賽？

B Sure, I'll go get my ball.
好的，我去拿我的球。

▶ 對話二

A Do you like basketball?
你喜歡籃球嗎？

B Yes, it's my favorite sport.
喜歡，那是我最喜歡的運動。

A There's a game tonight.
今晚有一場比賽。

B Yes, I know.
我知道。

A I have an extra ticket.
我多一張票。

Would you like to go?
你要不要去？

B Yes! I would love to go!
好，我很樂意去。

英語會話單字

☑ **sport** [sport] 運動

☑ **basketball** [ˈbæskɪtˌbɔl] 籃球

☑ **extra** [ˈɛkstrə] 額外的；多餘的

MEMO

Chapter 9

保健英語

Unit 35

I have a headache.
我頭很痛。

對話一 　　　　　　　　　　　　　　　　MP3-36

A Are you sick?
你在生病嗎？

B Yes, I have the flu.
是，我得了流行性感冒。

A Have you seen a doctor?
你有沒有去看醫生？

B Yes, he told me to rest for the next few days.
看了，他要我休息幾天。

對話二

A Are you feeling all right?
你覺得好嗎？

B No, I have a headache.
不好，我頭很痛。

A Would you like some Aspirin?
你要阿斯匹靈嗎？

B Yes, Please.
好。

純美語解說

　flu 是比 cold 更嚴重的感冒，說到 flu 時，都是在 flu 前面加個「the」，說法就是「the flu」，例如：「我有流行性感冒。」英語的說法就是「I have the flu.」。

會話靈活練習

▶ 家人病了

A Would you like me to take you to the doctor?
你要我帶你去看醫生嗎？

B Yes.
好。

▶ 朋友病了

A I'll buy you some cold medicine.
我會替你買一些感冒藥。

B Thank you. I appreciate it.
謝謝你。

* 美國人要謝謝別人為他做了某件事情時，常常在「Thank you.」後面再多加一句 「I appreciate it.」。

▶ 看過醫生之後

A What did the doctor tell you?
醫生跟你說什麼？

Chapter 9

B He said that I should take vitamin C.
他說我應該吃維他命 C。

➡️ 問候朋友的病情

A Do you feel better today?
你今天好一點了嗎？

B Yes, I feel much better.
是，我覺得好多了。

英語會話單字

☑ flu	[flu]	流行性感冒
☑ rest	[rɛst]	休息
☑ headache	[ˈhɛdˌek]	頭痛
☑ medicine	[ˈmɛdəsn̩]	醫藥
☑ vitamin	[ˈvaɪtəmɪn]	維他命
☑ doctor	[ˈdɑktɚ]	醫生

Unit 36

Do you need some medicine?
你要吃藥嗎？

 MP3-37

▶ 對話一

A How is your grandmother?
你祖母好嗎？

B She's ill.
她在生病。

A Why is she ill?
她為什麼生病？

B She has pneumonia.
她有肺炎。

A Oh, I hope she gets better.
噢，我希望她好一點。

▶ 對話二

A You look sick.
你看起來是病了。

B I don't feel well.
我覺得不舒服。

A Would you like some hot tea?
你要熱茶嗎？

It will make you feel better.
熱茶會讓你覺得舒服一些。

B Yes, that would be nice.
好，那很好。

Thank you.
謝謝你。

純美語解說

「drug」和「medicine」這兩個字都是「生病時吃的藥」，但是「drug」這個字還有「毒品」的意思，所以說到「drug」的時候要小心看整句話的意思，以辨明「drug」是在說「生病時吃的藥」還是「毒品」。曾經有一陣子美國發起反毒運動，有一個標題寫的是「Say no to drugs」，結果有人把這句話翻譯成「對『成藥』說不」，那可就相差十萬八千里了，美國人是在反毒品，而不是在反「成藥」。注意：「成藥」的英語是「over-the-counter medicine」，因為成藥是不需經過醫生處方，在美國商店的櫃子上就可以買到，所以叫做「over-the-counter medicine」。成藥的相反詞是「醫生處方的藥」，英語是「prescription medicine」。

會話靈活練習

▶ 問要不要吃藥

A Do you need some medicine?
你要吃藥嗎？

B No, thanks.
不用，謝謝你。

➡ 關懷朋友的感冒

A Are you taking something for your cold?
你有沒有吃什麼治療感冒的東西？

B Yes, I'm drinking a lot of orange juice.
有，我喝很多柳橙汁。

➡ 問有沒有去看醫生

A Have you been to a doctor?
你有沒有去看醫生？

B Yes, I went yesterday.
有，昨天去看過了。

➡ 問有沒有阿斯匹靈

A Do you have any Aspirin?
你有沒有阿斯匹靈？

B Yes, would you like some?
有，你要一些嗎？

➡ 喉嚨痛

A I have a sore throat.
我的喉嚨痛。

B You should buy some cough drops.
你應該買一些咳嗽滴劑。

☑ pneumonia	[njuˈmonjə]	肺炎
☑ feel	[fil]	感覺
☑ better	[ˈbɛtɚ]	較好的;更好
☑ cold	[kold]	n. 感冒
☑ orange	[ˈɔrɪndʒ]	柳橙
☑ juice	[dʒus]	果汁
☑ sore	[sor]	酸痛
☑ throat	[θrot]	喉嚨
☑ cough	[kɔf]	咳嗽
☑ drops	[drɑps]	n. 滴劑

Unit 37

I think I have a fever.
我想我在發燒。

對話一 MP3-38

A Are you all right?
你還好吧？

B I have a stomachache.
我的胃在痛。

A You should take some antacid.
你應該吃一些抗酸藥。

B Do you have any?
你有嗎？

A Yes, would you like some?
有，你要一些嗎？

B Please.
請給我一些。

 對話二

A I don't feel well.
我覺得不舒服。

I think I have a fever.
我想我在發燒。

B If you have a fever, you should see a doctor.
如果你在發燒，應該去看醫生。

Chapter 9

A Yes, I think I will.
是，我想我會去。

B I'll take you.
我帶你去。

第 10 單元說過「take」這個動詞有很多用法，如果要量體溫，也是用「take」這個字，就是「take temperature」，例如：「護士幫我量了體溫。」英語就是「The nurse took my temperature.」。

▶生病

A I feel really sick.
我覺得很不舒服。

B Let me take your temperature.
我來幫你量體溫。

▶胃痛

A Are you okay?
你還好吧？

B My stomach feels horrible.
我的胃很不舒服。

▶生病

A How have you been?
你最近好嗎？

B I've been sick all week.
我已經病了一整個星期。

▶ 想量體溫

A Do you have a thermometer?
你有沒有溫度計？

B Yes, I do.
有，我有。

▶ 生病

A I feel horrible.
我覺得很不舒服。

B You should stay in bed.
你應該留在床上。

英語會話單字

☑ **stomachache** [ˈstʌməkˌek] 胃痛

☑ **antacid** [æntˈæsɪd] 解酸劑；抗酸劑

☑ **fever** [ˈfivɚ] 發燒

☑ **temperature** [ˈtɛmpərətʃɚ] 體溫

☑ **thermometer** [θəˈmɑmətɚ] 溫度計

☑ **stomach** [ˈstʌmək] 胃

☑ **horrible** [ˈhɔrəbl̩] （口語）糟透的；可怕的

☑ **stay** [ste] 停留

Chapter 9

Unit 38

Is your flu gone yet?
你感冒好了嗎？

▶ 對話一 MP3-39

A That's a bad cough.
你咳得很厲害。

B I've been coughing all weekend.
我已經咳了一整個週末。

A You probably have bronchitis.
你可能有支氣管炎。

B I should make an appointment with the clinic.
你應該跟診所約個時間去看看。

▶ 對話二

A Did you go to the clinic?
你有沒有去診所？

B Yes, I have pneumonia.
去過了，我有肺炎。

A Did they give you some medicine?
他們有沒有給你藥？

B They gave me some antibiotics.
他們給我一些抗生素。

會話靈活練習

▶ 問候朋友的病情

A Are you still feeling sick?
你還在生病嗎？

B Yes, the doctor told me to stay in bed for a few days.
是，醫生要我在床上多休息幾天。

▶ 問候朋友的病情

A Is your flu gone yet?
你感冒好了嗎？

B No, but I'm getting better.
還沒，但是我現在好多了。

▶ 問候朋友的病情

A How long have you been sick?
你病了多久？

B I've been sick for about two days.
已經病了約兩天。

▶ 問候朋友的病情

A How's your stomach?
你的胃現在怎麼樣？

B It's fine.
還好。

➡️ 問候朋友的病情

A Are you feeling better than last week?
你比上星期好一點了嗎？

B Yes, much better.
是，好多了。

英語會話單字

☐ bronchitis	[brɑnˈkaɪtɪs]	支氣管炎
☐ appointment	[əˈpɔɪntmənt]	約定時間
☐ clinic	[ˈklɪnɪk]	診所
☐ pneumonia	[njuˈmonjə]	肺炎
☐ medicine	[ˈmɛdəsn̩]	醫藥
☐ antibiotics	[ˌæntɪbaɪˈɑtɪks]	抗生素
☐ flu	[flu]	流行性感冒

Chapter 10

休假英語

Unit 39

I'd like to call in sick.
我打電話來請病假。

▶ 對話一   🔘 MP3-40

A Can I help you?
你有什麼事嗎？

B Yes. This is John Smith.
有，我叫約翰史密斯。

I would like to leave a message.
我想留個話。

A All right.
好的。

B Please inform Mr. White that I am sick.
請你告訴懷特先生說我病了。

▶ 對話二

A Hello. Mr. Smith?
哈囉，史密斯先生嗎？

B Yes, can I help you?
是的，有什麼事嗎？

A This is John.
我是約翰。

B Hello John.
哈囉，約翰。

　　Is everything all right?
　　一切都好嗎？

A No, I'm very ill.
　　不，我病得很嚴重。

　　I won't be able to come in today.
　　我今天沒辦法來上班。

B All right then.
　　那沒關係。

　　Call me if you're still sick tomorrow.
　　如果你明天還生病，打個電話給我。

純美語解說

　　「make it」這個片語的意思是「能夠去某個已經安排好的活動或場合」。若你一早起來，人很不舒服，於是你打電話跟老闆請假，這時你可以說：「I'm not going to make it in today.」（我今天不能來上班。）或是「I won't be able to make it.」。

　　打電話請病假的英語就是「call in sick」，若你生病了，打電話到公司去，你可以告訴有關人員說：「I'd like to call in sick.」（我打電話來請病假。）

會話靈活練習

▶ **請病假的說法之一**

A Hi. I'd like to call in sick.
　　嗨，我打電話來請病假。

B I'll let Mr. Smith know.
　　我會告訴史密斯先生。

請病假的說法之二

A I'm very sick.
我病得很嚴重。

I won't be coming in today.
我今天不能來。

B That's fine.
沒關係。

請病假的說法之三

A I have the flu.
我得了感冒。

I won't be in this weekend.
這個週末我不去。

B All right, then I'll see you Monday.
好的，那星期一見。

請病假的說法之四

A I'm not feeling well.
我覺得不舒服。

I won't be able to make it.
我沒辦法來。

B I'm sorry to hear that.
聽到這個消息，我真遺憾。

I'll see you tomorrow then.
那明天見。

▶ 請病假的說法之五

A Hello. Please tell Mr. Smith that I won't be in today.
哈囉，請告訴史密斯先生我今天不能來。

I'm sick.
我病了。

B All right. I'll tell him.
好的，我會告訴他。

英語會話單字

☑ leave	[liv]	留著
☑ message	['mɛsɪdʒ]	留言
☑ inform	[ɪn'fɔrm]	通知；告知
☑ still	[stɪl]	仍然
☑ weekend	['wik'ɛnd]	週末

I won't be able to come in today.
我今天不能來。

MP3-41

 對話一

A Hi. Mr. White?
嗨，是懷特先生嗎？

B Yes?
你是誰？

A This is John.
我是約翰。

I won't be able to come in today.
我今天不能來。

B Oh? What's wrong?
是嗎？怎麼啦？

A My wife is in the hospital.
我太太在醫院。

對話二

A Hello. Is this Richard?
哈囉，是理查嗎？

B Yes, it is.
是的。

A This is Mary.
我是瑪莉。

I can't come in.
我不能來上班。

My car broke down.
我的車子壞了。

B I'm sorry to hear that.
聽到這個消息，我真遺憾。

A I may come in tomorrow.
我明天可能會來。

B All right, I'll see you tomorrow.
好的，明天見。

純美語解說

　　用英語講電話時，由於在電話中彼此看不到對方，所以當你跟對方説「我是某某人」時，不是説「I am 某某人.」，而是説「This is 某某人.」。同樣地，當你問對方是某某人嗎，不是問「Are you 某某人？」，而是説「Is this 某某人？」。

　　當對方問你是某某人嗎，而你正好是對方問的人，英語的回答不是「Yes, I am.」，而是「Yes, it is.」。

會話靈活練習

▶ **請事假的說法之一**

A I won't be coming in.
我不能來。

I have some personal matters to take care of.
我有一些私人的事情要處理。

B I'll tell Mr. White.
我會告訴懷特先生。

▶ 請事假的說法之二

A I can't make it today.
我今天不能來。

I have an emergency to take care of.
有一個緊急事件要處理。

B Ok, well, let me know when you can return.
好，那你能來的時候再通知我。

▶ 請事假的說法之三

A I have a family emergency.
我家裡有緊急事件。

I'm not able to come in today.
我今天不能來。

B I'll give Mr. Smith your message.
我會把你的話轉達給史密斯先生。

▶ 請事假的說法之四

A My wife is very ill.
我太太病得很嚴重。

I can't come in today.
我今天不能來。

I'll be in tomorrow.
我明天會來。

B Ok, see you then.
好，再見。

▶ **請事假的說法之五**

A I'm not coming in tomorrow.
我明天不來。

I have to attend a funeral.
我必須去參加一個葬禮。

B All right, I'll expect to see you Wednesday.
好，星期三再見。

英語會話單字

☑ hospital	[ˈhɑspɪtl̩]	醫院
☑ personal	[ˈpɝsənl̩]	私人的
☑ matter	[ˈmætɚ]	事情
☑ emergency	[ɪˈmɝdʒənsɪ]	緊急事件
☑ return	[rɪˈtɝn]	返回
☑ message	[ˈmɛsɪdʒ]	留言
☑ attend	[əˈtɛnd]	參加
☑ funeral	[ˈfjunərəl]	喪禮
☑ expect	[ɪkˈspɛkt]	期待

Chapter 10

Unit 41

I'm taking my vacation next week.
我下星期要休假。

●MP3-42

▶ 對話一

A I'm taking my vacation next week.
我下星期要休假。

B Where are you vacationing?
你要去哪裡度假？

A I'm going to Greece.
我要去希臘。

I'll be gone for two weeks.
我要去兩個星期。

B We'll see you when you get back.
等你回來再見。

▶ 對話二

A When are you planning on taking your vacation?
你計畫什麼時候休假？

B I'm planning on taking my vacation next month.
我計畫下個月休假。

A Ok, I'll change the schedule then.
好，那我會改一改進度表。

B Thank you.
謝謝你。

會話靈活練習

建議休假的時間

A Would you like to take your vacation this month?
你要在這個月休假嗎？

B Yes, that would be great.
好，那很好。

要休假

A I'd like to take my vacation this month.
我這個月要休假。

B That should be fine.
那很好。

安排休假的時間

A Could you wait until next week to take your vacation?
你可以等到下星期再休假嗎？

B Sure, that shouldn't be a problem.
好，應該沒問題。

▶ 宣布要去度假

A I'm leaving tomorrow for vacation.
我明天要去度假。

B Ok, enjoy yourself.
好,祝你玩得愉快。

▶ 問休假的時間

A Are you going to take your vacation this month?
你這個月要休假嗎?

B No, I plan on taking my vacation next month.
不,我計畫下個月休假。

英語會話單字

☑ plan	[plæn]	計畫
☑ change	[tʃendʒ]	改變
☑ schedule	[ˈskɛdʒʊl]	時間表;行程;進度
☑ wait	[wet]	等
☑ until	[ʌnˈtɪl]	直到
☑ problem	[ˈprɑbləm]	問題

I can't come to work.
我不能來上班。

> 對話一   🔘 MP3-43

A My car broke down.
我的車子壞了。

     I won't be able to make it to work.
     我沒辦法發動我的車子。

B Are you having your car repaired?
你的車子在修理嗎？

A Yes, It's in the garage now.
是，現在在修車廠。

B When will it be ready?
什麼時候會好？

A It should be ready by tomorrow morning.
明天早上應該會好。

> 對話二

A I've been injured.
我受傷了。

     I'm not able to work today.
     我今天沒辦法來上班。

B Is it serious?
傷得很嚴重嗎？

A Yes, I broke my leg.
是，我的腿斷了。

B I'm sorry to hear that.
聽到這個消息，我真遺憾。

A I may not be in for a while.
我可能要請假一段時間。

純美語解說

　　當有人告訴你任何壞消息時，你只要以「I'm sorry to hear that.」這句話回答對方就沒錯！任何時候美國人只要聽到壞消息，一定是先跟對方說「I'm sorry to hear that.」，然後再說其他的。

會話靈活練習

▶ 出了車禍

A I can't come in.
我不能來。

　　I got into a car accident.
　　我出了車禍。

B I hope you're all right.
我希望你沒事。

▶ 太太快要生產

A I'm not able to come to work today.
我今天不能來上班。

My wife's in labor.
我太太快生了。

B I understand.
我可以瞭解。

女兒受傷

A I'm calling to let you know that I won't be coming in.
我打電話來告訴你，我不能來。

My daughter injured herself.
我女兒受傷了。

B All right then.
那沒關係。

I hope she's O.K.
我希望她沒事。

請假

A Please tell the manager that I can't come in to work.
請告訴經理，我不能來上班。

B I'll do that.
我會的。

輪胎破了

A I can't come to work.
我不能來上班。

One of my tires blew out.
我有一個輪胎破了。

B All right, come in as soon as you can.
好，你修好就儘快來。

英語會話單字

☑ repair	[rɪˈpɛr]	修理
☑ garage	[gəˈrɑʒ]	修車廠
☑ ready	[ˈrɛdɪ]	準備好
☑ injure	[ˈɪndʒɚ]	受傷
☑ serious	[ˈsɪrɪəs]	嚴重的
☑ broke	[brok]	斷了（break 的過去式）
☑ leg	[lɛg]	腿
☑ accident	[ˈæksədənt]	車禍；交通事故
☑ labor	[ˈlebɚ]	（生產前的）陣痛
☑ manager	[ˈmænɪdʒɚ]	經理
☑ tire	[taɪr]	輪胎
☑ understand	[ˌʌndɚˈstænd]	瞭解；明白

Chapter 11

租屋英語

I'm looking for a two bedroom.
我在找兩房的公寓。

 MP3-44

▶ 對話一

A Do you know where I could find an apartment?
你知道我到哪裡可以找到住的公寓嗎？

B What are you looking for?
你在找怎麼樣的公寓？

A I'm looking for a two bedroom.
我在找兩房的公寓。

B I have a friend who's moving out of a two bedroom.
我有一個朋友正要搬出一間兩房的公寓。

A Would you give me your friend's number?
你可以把你朋友的電話號碼給我嗎？

B Sure.
好的。

▶ 對話二

A I'm looking for an apartment.
我在找公寓。

Where should I start?
我應該從哪裡開始找？

B You should look in the apartment guide.
你應該找公寓指南。

A Where can I find that?
我到哪裡可以找得到？

B Try looking at the grocery store.
到雜貨店試試看。

A All right, thanks.
好，謝謝你。

純美語解說

「a two bedroom」就是「a two-bedroom apartment」。「two-bedroom apartment」的意思是「兩個房間的公寓」，而「一間兩房的公寓」，英語就是「a two-bedroom apartment」。

會話靈活練習

尋找公寓

A I really need to find an apartment.
我真的需要找間公寓。

Do you have any ideas?
你有什麼主意嗎？

B No, but I'll ask my friends.
沒有，但是我可以問問朋友。

尋找公寓

A Where can I find a good apartment?
我到哪裡可以找到一間好的公寓？

B There is a nice apartment complex near where I live.
我住的附近有個不錯的公寓區。

▶ 尋找公寓

A Do you know where I should look?
你知道我該到哪裡找嗎？

B You should look in the paper.
你應該在報上找找看。

▶ 尋找便宜的住所

A I need to find a cheap place to live.
我需要找個便宜的地方住。

B I know a place nearby.
我知道附近有個地方。

英語會話單字

☑ apartment	[ə'pɑrtmənt]	公寓
☑ bedroom	['bɛd͵rum]	臥室
☑ friend	[frɛnd]	朋友
☑ start	[stɑrt]	開始
☑ guide	[gaɪd]	指南；手冊
☑ grocery	['grosərɪ]	雜貨
☑ idea	[aɪ'diə]	概念
☑ complex	['kɑmplɛks]	（有同一性質的建築的）一區
☑ cheap	[tʃip]	便宜的

Unit 44

How much is the apartment?
租一間公寓要多少錢？

 MP3-45

▶ 對話一

A Hello. What is the price on your two-bedroom apartments?
哈囉，你們的兩房公寓要多少錢？

B The two bedrooms are $440 per month.
兩房公寓一個月是四百四十元。

A Does that come with a washer and dryer?
公寓裡有洗衣機和烘乾機嗎？

B Yes, that does.
有。

▶ 對話二

A I'm calling about the one-bedroom apartment.
我想問一些有關那間一房公寓的問題。

B Yes, how can I help you?
好，你要問什麼？

A I would like to know whether the apartment is furnished.
我想知道那間公寓有沒有家具。

B No, it's not.
沒有。

▶ 問一些有關你想租的公寓的情況

A Is the apartment in a good neighborhood?
這間公寓在好的住宅區裡嗎？

B Yes, it is.
是的。

▶ 問一些有關你想租的公寓的情況

A Is there a bus stop nearby?
附近有公車站嗎？

B There's one on the corner.
轉角處有一個。

▶ 問一些有關你想租的公寓的情況

A How much is the apartment?
租一間公寓要多少錢？

B The apartment is $240 per month.
租一間公寓一個月是兩百四十元。

▶ 問一些有關你想租的公寓的情況

A Is there a store near the apartment building?
公寓大樓附近有沒有商店？

B Yes, there is a shopping center down the road.
有，再過去一點有一個購物中心。

▶ 問一些有關你想租的公寓的情況

A Which floor is the apartment on?
這間公寓在幾樓？

B The apartment is on the third floor.
這間公寓在三樓。

英語會話單字

☑ price	[praɪs]	價格
☑ washer	['waʃɚ]	洗衣機
☑ dryer	['draɪɚ]	烘乾機
☑ whether	['hwɛðɚ]	是否
☑ furnished	['fɜnɪʃt]	配備家具的
☑ neighborhood	['nebɚˌhʊd]	鄰近地區
☑ stop	[stɑp]	停車站
☑ corner	['kɔrnɚ]	角落
☑ building	['bɪldɪŋ]	大樓；建築物
☑ road	[rod]	路

What's your price range?
你多少錢要租？

🔘 MP3-46

▶ 對話一

A I need to find a one-bedroom apartment.
我需要找一間一房的公寓。

B There is a one bedroom next door to me.
我的隔壁有一間。

A Does it have a dishwasher?
那一間有洗碗機嗎？

B Yes, I think it does.
有，我想應該有。

▶ 對話二

A Where can I find a furnished one-bedroom apartment?
我到哪裡可以找到一間有家具的一房公寓？

B What's your price range?
你多少錢要租？

A I don't want to spend more than $500 per month.
我一個月不想花超過五百元。

B Is there a specific location you would like?
一定要哪個地點嗎？

A Yes, I'd like to find something near the university.
是，我想找大學附近的地方。

會話靈活練習

▶ 告訴朋友你在找什麼樣的公寓

A I need to find a large two-bedroom apartment.
我需要找一間大的兩房公寓。

B I'll help you look.
我會幫你留意。

▶ 告訴朋友你在找什麼樣的公寓

A I want to find something near where I work.
我要在我上班的附近找個住的地方。

B That shouldn't be a problem.
應該沒有問題。

▶ 告訴朋友你在找什麼樣的公寓

A I would like something on the second floor.
我想要找一間在二樓的公寓。

B Really?
真的？

There's a vacant apartment above mine.
我的樓上有一間空的公寓。

▶ 告訴朋友你在找什麼樣的公寓

A Do you know what you're looking for?
你知道你在找什麼樣的公寓嗎？

B Yes, I'd like something in a quiet neighborhood.
是的，我想要在安靜一點的社區的。

▶ 告訴朋友你在找什麼樣的公寓

A How much can you pay?
你可以付多少錢？

B No more than $300.
不超過三百元。

英語會話單字

☑ dishwasher	[ˈdɪʃˌwɑʃɚ]	洗碗機
☑ price	[praɪs]	價格
☑ range	[rendʒ]	範圍
☑ spend	[spɛnd]	花錢
☑ specific	[spɪˈsɪfɪk]	特定的
☑ location	[loˈkeʃən]	地點
☑ university	[ˌjunəˈvɝsətɪ]	大學
☑ problem	[ˈprɑbləm]	問題
☑ second	[ˈsɛkənd]	第二
☑ vacant	[ˈvekənt]	空著的
☑ quiet	[ˈkwaɪət]	安靜的

Unit 46 Does the rent include utilities?
租金包括水電、瓦斯費嗎？

🔘 MP3-47

 對話一

A How long is the lease for?
租約是多久？

B Nine months.
九個月。

A Is a security deposit required?
需要保證金嗎？

B Yes, you will need to pay a deposit of $100.
要，你要付一百元的保證金。

 對話二

A Will I get my deposit back at the end of the lease?
租約期滿，你會退還我的訂金嗎？

B Yes, if the apartment is undamaged.
會，如果公寓沒有損壞的話。

A Does your rent include utilities?
房租包括水電、瓦斯費嗎？

B No, you are responsible for the utilities.
不，水電、瓦斯費你要自己負責。

「utility」這個字是指「瓦斯、水電等的供應」，所以當你要租房子時，你想知道對方的房租裡有沒有包括水電、瓦斯費，英語的問法就是「Does your rent include utilities?」。

會話靈活練習

▶ 問租金情形

A Does the rent include utilities?
租金包括水電、瓦斯費嗎？

B Yes, utilities are included.
是的，包括水電、瓦斯費。

▶ 問租期

A When does the lease end?
租約什麼時候結束？

B The lease ends in April.
租約四月結束。

▶ 找便宜的公寓

A What is your cheapest apartment?
你們最便宜的公寓是什麼？

B We have an efficiency for $200 per month.
我們有公寓小套間，一個月兩百元。

▶ 問有沒有便宜一點的

A Do you have something more economic?
你有沒有便宜一點的公寓？

B No, the two-bedroom apartments are a fixed price.
沒有，兩房的公寓價格是固定的。

▶ 問有沒有便宜一點的

A Is this your cheapest apartment?
這是你們最便宜的公寓嗎？

B Yes, it is.
是的。

英語會話單字

☐ lease	[lis]	出租
☐ security	[sɪ'kjʊrətɪ]	保證；擔保
☐ deposit	[dɪ'pɑzɪt]	訂金；保證金
☐ require	[rɪ'kwaɪr]	要求
☐ end	[ɛnd]	結束
☐ undamaged	[ʌn'dæmɪdʒɪd]	沒有損壞
☐ utility	[ju'tɪlətɪ]	水電、瓦斯
☐ responsible	[rɪ'spɑnsəbl̩]	有責任的；負責的
☐ rent	[rɛnt]	租金
☐ include	[ɪn'klud]	包括

Chapter 11

☑ efficiency	[əˈfɪʃənsɪ]	公寓小套間（只有一個房間、小廚房、小浴室）
☑ economic	[ˌikəˈnɑmɪk]	節約的；省儉的
☑ fixed	[fɪkst]	固定的

Chapter 12

資訊英語

When is the baseball game starting?
棒球賽幾點開始？

 MP3-48

 對話一

A Hello. What time is "Star Wars" playing?
哈囉，「星際大戰」什麼時候上映？

B That shows at seven o'clock.
七點上映。

A Do you have a student discount?
你有沒有賣學生票？

B Yes, we do.
有。

It's three dollars with the discount.
學生打折票是三塊錢。

A Thank you.
謝謝你。

對話二

A Excuse me. Do you still have front row tickets?
對不起，你們還有前排座位的票嗎？

B Yes, we do.
有，還有。

A How much are they?
多少錢？

B Those are seventy-five dollars.
七十五塊錢。

會話靈活練習

▶ 問球賽的時間

A Can I help you?
有什麼事嗎？

B Yes, I need to know what time the game starts.
是，我需要知道球賽何時開始。

▶ 問有沒有前排座位的票

A Is front row seating still available?
你們還有前排座位的票嗎？

B I'm sorry, but the front row is sold out.
對不起，前排座位的票都賣光了。

▶ 問球賽開始的時間

A Excuse me, when is the baseball game starting?
對不起，棒球賽幾點開始？

B The game is starting at six o'clock.
球賽六點開始。

▶ 問時間

A Excuse me, do you have the correct time?
對不起，你知道現在的時間嗎？

B Yes, it's now eight thirty.
知道，現在是八點半。

▶ 問戲院在哪裡

A Could you tell me where the theater is?
請你告訴我戲院在哪裡好嗎？

B Yes, it's two blocks down on your right.
好，再走兩個街段，就在你的右邊。

英語會話單字

☑ show	[ʃo]	（電影）放映
☑ discount	[ˈdɪskaʊnt]	折扣；打折
☑ front	[frʌnt]	前面的
☑ seating	[ˈsitɪŋ]	座位
☑ available	[əˈveləbḷ]	有得賣的；可得的
☑ row	[ro]	排
☑ correct	[kəˈrɛkt]	正確的
☑ theater	[ˈθiətɚ]	戲院
☑ block	[blɑk]	（市區裡）街段

Unit 48

I'd like to rent a car.
我要租部車子。

對話一　　　　　　　　　　　　　　　　　　MP3-49

A Hi. I'd like to rent a car.
嗨，我要租部車子。

B What are you interested in?
你要租什麼車？

A I would like something economical.
我要租便宜一點的。

B All right, how long do you need it?
好的，你需要多久？

A I'll need the car for two weeks.
我需要租兩個星期。

對話二

A I would like to rent a car for the weekend.
我要租一部車子，這個週末要用。

B What would you like?
你想要什麼樣的車？

A I need something that is gas efficient.
我需要省油一點的。

B We have several smaller cars which are very cheap on gas.
我們有好幾部小車子，用油都很省。

▶ 問租車資料

A How can I help you?
有什麼事嗎？

B I would like some information about car rentals.
我需要一些有關租車的資料。

▶ 要租車

A I would like to rent a German import.
我想要租一部德國進口車。

B We have many to choose from.
我們有很多可以選。

▶ 說明租車時間

A Can I be of assistance?
需要我幫什麼忙嗎？

B I need a car for the next couple of days.
我需要租一部車，要租兩、三天。

▶ 要租車

A I would like to rent a car.
我要租一部車。

　 Do you accept checks?
　 你們收支票嗎？

B I'm sorry, but we can't take checks.
對不起，我們不收支票。

▶ 問租車期限

A How long can I rent a car?
我租一部車可以租多久？

B There is a one month limit.
最久可以租到一個月。

英語會話單字

☑ rent	[rɛnt]	出租；租金
☑ economical	[ˌikə'nɑmɪkl̩]	經濟的；省儉的
☑ gas	[gæs]	汽油
☑ efficient	[ə'fɪʃənt]	效率高的
☑ cheap	[tʃip]	便宜的
☑ information	[ˌɪnfɚ'meʃən]	資料；資訊；訊息
☑ rental	['rɛntl̩]	出租
☑ import	[ɪm'port]	進口
☑ assistance	[ə'sɪstəns]	協助；幫助
☑ couple	['kʌpl̩]	一對
☑ limit	['lɪmɪt]	限制

Unit 49

What time does flight 302 arrive?

302 號班機什麼時候到？

🎵 MP3-50

▶ 對話一

A I need to know when the next flight to Tokyo leaves.
我需要知道下一班到東京的班機幾時離開。

B The next flight is at 1:35 P.M.
下一班飛機是下午一點三十五分。

A Are there any openings?
還有沒有座位？

B Yes, there is one opening in row 35A.
有，35A 有一個座位。

A Could you reserve it for me?
你可以幫我訂下來嗎？

B Certainly.
好的。

▶ 對話二

A Hello. Could I reserve a flight?
哈囉，我可以預訂一個機位嗎？

B Certainly. What is your destination?
可以，你要去哪裡？

194

A New York.
紐約。

B There is a flight leaving March 15th.
有一班飛機三月十五日起飛。

Would you like me to reserve it?
你要我幫你訂下來嗎？

A Yes, please.
好的，請幫我訂下來。

會話靈活練習

▶ 問班機的資料

A How may I help you?
有什麼事嗎？

B I need flight information.
我需要班機的資料。

▶ 問班機的資料

A Is there a flight leaving for Hong Kong today?
今天有沒有班機飛香港？

B Yes, that flight is scheduled for 3:45.
有，那一班是在三點四十五分。

➡ 問班機到達時間

A What time does flight 302 arrive?
302 號班機什麼時候到？

B That flight is due to arrive in fifteen minutes.
該班飛機還有十五分到。

➡ 要訂機位

A Could I make a reservation for flight 205?
我可以訂 205 號班機的機位嗎？

B I'm sorry, but that flight is booked up.
對不起，該班飛機都訂滿了。

英語會話單字

☑ flight	[flaɪt]	班機
☑ leave	[liv]	離開
☑ opening	[ˈopənɪŋ]	空位
☑ reserve	[rɪˈzɝv]	預訂
☑ certainly	[ˈsɝtn̩lɪ]	當然；當然可以
☑ destination	[ˌdɛstəˈneʃən]	目的地
☑ schedule	[ˈskɛdʒʊl]	安排時間
☑ behind	[bɪˈhaɪnd]	在～的後面
☑ delay	[dɪˈle]	拖延；耽擱
☑ arrive	[əˈraɪv]	抵達
☑ reservation	[ˌrɛzɚˈveʃən]	v. 預訂
☑ book	[bʊk]	v. 預訂

Unit 50

How much is admission?
入場券要多少錢？

 對話一   📀 MP3-51

A Hello. I need tour information.
哈囉，我需要嚮導帶領參觀的資料。

B Certainly.
好的。

We give tours of the castle every Thursday at nine.
每個星期四九點我們有嚮導帶領參觀古堡。

A What is the price of admission?
入場券要多少錢？

B Are you a student?
你是學生嗎？

A Yes, I am.
是的。

B Admission will be five dollars.
入場券要五塊錢。

 對話二

A When is the next tour of the Louvre?
下一次嚮導帶領參觀羅浮宮是什麼時候？

B That will be three o'clock today.
是今天三點鐘。

A May I bring a camera?
我可以帶照相機來嗎？

B No, cameras are not allowed.
不可以，不准帶照相機。

純美語解說

在一些給人參觀的博物館、古堡或歷史建築物等等，有些地方會設有嚮導帶領遊客一邊說明，一邊遊覽，英語叫做「tour」。通常一天裡 tour 的時間是固定的，例如，每一小時有一個 tour 開始，或是某個時間開始 tour，所以若你到了這種有 tour 的地方參觀，第一件事就是問 tour 的時間。

會話靈活練習

▶ 問有沒有嚮導帶領參觀

A Do you hold tours?
你們有沒有嚮導帶領參觀？

B Yes, we hold tours every Saturday.
有，每星期六我們有嚮導帶領參觀。

▶ 問入場券的價錢

A How much is admission?
入場券要多少錢？

B Ten dollars.
十塊錢。

▶ 問展出期限

A How long will you be showing the Van Gogh exhibit?
雨果的作品展，將會展覽多久？

B The exhibit will be here until April.
將會展覽到四月。

▶ 問有沒有導遊帶領參觀

A Will you be giving tours today?
你們今天有嚮導帶領參觀嗎？

B I'm sorry, but the museum is closed for today.
很抱歉，博物館今天沒開。

▶ 導遊帶領參觀需時多久

A How long will the tour last?
嚮導帶領參觀一次需時多久？

B The tour is one hour long.
嚮導帶領參觀一次是一個小時。

英語會話單字

☐ **tour**	[tʊr]	旅遊
☐ **castle**	[ˈkæsl̩]	古堡
☐ **admission**	[ədˈmɪʃən]	入場費

Chapter 12

199

☐ camera	[ˈkæmərə]	相機
☐ allow	[əˈlaʊ]	允許
☐ hold	[hold]	舉辦
☐ exhibit	[ɪɡˈzɪbɪt]	展覽
☐ last	[læst]	延續；持續

Chapter 13

科技英語

Unit 51

Do you use e-mail?
你使用電子郵件嗎？

對話一 MP3-52

A Do you use e-mail?
你使用電子郵件嗎？

B Yes, it's cheaper than using the phone.
有，那比用電話便宜。

A Could I get your e-mail address?
請給我你的電子郵件地址。

B Sure.
好。

對話二

A Do you have a computer?
你有電腦嗎？

B Yes, I use it for word processing.
有，我用它來做文字處理。

How about you?
你呢？

A I use the terminals on campus.
我使用學校的電腦終端機。

B Can you print from those terminals?
從那些終端機上可以列印嗎？

A Yes.
可以。

會話靈活練習

▶ 電子郵件聯絡

A What's the best way to contact you?
我如何跟你聯絡最好？

B You can contact me through e-mail.
你可以用電子郵件跟我聯絡。

▶ 想借用電腦

A Can I use your computer this weekend?
這個週末我可以借用你的電腦嗎？

B That's fine.
沒問題。

▶ 談電腦螢幕

A What kind of monitor do you have?
你的螢幕是哪一種？

B I have a color monitor.
我的是彩色螢幕。

▶ 談網際網路

A Do you use the internet?
你使用網際網路嗎？

B Yes, it's very useful.
是，它很有用。

▶ 要買部新電腦

A Are you going to upgrade your computer?
你要把你的電腦升級嗎？

B No, I'm going to buy a new one.
不，我要買部新電腦。

英語會話單字

☐ cheaper	[ˈtʃipɚ]	較便宜的
☐ phone	[fon]	電話
☐ address	[ˈædrɛs]	n. 地址
☐ computer	[kəmˈpjutɚ]	電腦
☐ terminal	[ˈtɜmənl]	電腦終端機
☐ print	[prɪnt]	印出
☐ contact	[ˈkɑntækt]	聯繫；聯絡
☐ through	[θru]	經由
☐ monitor	[ˈmɑnətɚ]	（電腦）螢幕
☐ color	[ˈkʌlɚ]	顏色
☐ Internet	[ˈɪntɚˌnɛt]	網際網路
☐ useful	[ˈjusfəl]	有用的；有助益的
☐ upgrade	[ˈʌpˈgred]	升級

Unit 52 Do you use the internet?
你使用網際網路嗎？

 對話一　　　　　　　　　　　　　　MP3-53

A Do you use the internet?
你使用網際網路嗎？

B Yes, I use the World Wide Web.
是的，我使用 WWW。

A Is that a good source of information?
那是找資訊的好來源嗎？

B Definitely, I can find more on the internet than anywhere else.
肯定是，我在網際網路上可以比在其他任何地方找到更多的資訊。

 對話二

A I need to buy some parts for my car.
我的車子需要買些零件。

B Did you know that you can shop on the internet?
你知不知道你可以在網際網路上買到？

A Really?
真的？

B Yes, you can order anything with on-line shopping.
是啊，你可以用線上購物訂購任何東西。

Chapter 13

電腦遊戲

A Do you play games on your computer?
你在電腦上玩電玩嗎？

B Yes, I have a library of games for my computer.
有，我收藏了很多電腦遊戲。

線上購物

A I'd like to order something over the internet.
我想要在網際網路上訂購東西。

B You can use my computer.
你可以用我的電腦。

下載資訊

A Does it take a long time to download information?
要下載資訊需要很久嗎？

B That depends on how fast your modem is.
那要看你的數據機的速度了。

談數據機

A Do you have a fast modem?
你的數據機速度很快嗎？

B No, I need to upgrade it.
沒有，我需要把它升級。

▶ 談硬碟機

A I'd like to install a second hard-drive.
我想要安裝第二個硬碟機。

B That should be easy.
那應該很容易。

英語會話單字

☑ source	[sors]	來源
☑ definitely	['dɛfənɪtlɪ]	確定地；肯定地
☑ part	[pɑrt]	零件
☑ shopping	['ʃɑpɪŋ]	購物
☑ game	[gem]	（球類）比賽；遊戲
☑ download	['daʊn'lod]	下載
☑ depend	[dɪ'pɛnd]	視～而定
☑ modem	['modəm]	數據機
☑ install	[ɪn'stɔl]	安裝；設置
☑ easy	['izɪ]	簡單的

Would you like to play a video game?
你要玩電動玩具嗎?

 MP3-54

▶ 對話一

A Would you like to go to the electronics store?
你要去電子商店嗎?

B Yes, there are a few video games I'd like to buy.
是,我要去買幾個電動玩具。

A Do you play a lot of video games?
你玩很多電動玩具嗎?

B Yes, I have three different game systems.
是,我有三種不同的遊戲系統。

▶ 對話二

A Would you like to play a video game?
你要玩電動玩具嗎?

B Sure.
好。

A I'll set the game on two player mode.
我來把它設定在兩個人可以玩的模式。

Here's a control.
控制器在這裡。

B What do I do?
我該怎麼辦？

A Practice until you learn what the buttons do.
練習到你知道這些按鈕是做什麼的。

會話靈活練習

▶ 談電動玩具

A Is this a difficult game?
這是很困難的遊戲嗎？

B No, but you should read the instructions.
不難，但是你必須看說明書。

▶ 談電動玩具的系統

A Did you buy this system recently?
你最近才買這個系統嗎？

B Yes, it's the fastest system available.
是的，這是市面上有的最快的系統。

▶ 談電動玩具

A Is this game multi-player?
這個遊戲可以好幾個人一起玩嗎？

B Yes, up to four people can play.
是，最多可以有四個人一起玩。

☑ electronics	[ɪˌlɛkˈtrɑnɪks]	電子產品
☑ video	[ˈvɪdɪˌo]	電視的
☑ system	[ˈsɪstəm]	系統
☑ set	[sɛt]	設定
☑ mode	[mod]	模式
☑ control	[kənˈtrol]	控制器
☑ practice	[ˈpræktɪs]	練習
☑ button	[ˈbʌtn̩]	按鈕
☑ difficult	[ˈdɪfəˌkʌlt]	困難的
☑ instructions	[ɪnˈstrʌkʃənz]	用法說明
☑ recently	[ˈrisn̩tlɪ]	最近地

Unit 54

Can I use your computer?
我可以借用你的電腦嗎？

 對話一

🔘 MP3-55

A Where can I type my paper?
有什麼地方我可以打我的報告？

B You can go to the computer lab.
你可以到電腦室去打。

A Where is that?
電腦室在哪裡？

B It's on the third floor of the campus library.
在學校圖書館的三樓。

 對話二

A I need to graph a project for my Physics lab.
我的物理課的實驗報告需要繪圖形。

B Do you have a graphing program?
你有繪圖軟體嗎？

A No.
沒有。

B You can find a graphing program in the computer lab.
電腦室裡有繪圖軟體。

A Could you show me how to use it?
你可以做給我看怎麼使用嗎？

B Sure.
好。

▶ 繪圖計算機

A Do I need a graphing calculator for this class?
這堂課我需要繪圖計算機嗎？

B No, you should use a scientific calculator.
不需要，你應該使用科學用的計算機。

▶ 談電腦程式語言

A Which programming languages do you know?
你知道哪些電腦程式語言？

B I know C and Pascal.
我知道 C 和 Pascal。

▶ 學電腦程式語言

A Which programming language should I learn first?
我應該先學哪一種電腦程式語言？

B You should probably start with C.
你可能應該先學 C。

▶ 電腦軟體

A I just bought a math program for my computer.
我剛買了一個給我的電腦用的數學軟體。

B That's a good idea.
那是個好主意。

▶ 網路的主頁

A Do you have a web page?
你在網路上有一個網頁嗎？

B Yes, I just completed it.
有，我才剛做完。

英語會話單字

☐ type	[taɪp]	打字
☐ lab	[læb]	實驗室
☐ graph	[græf]	圖形；圖像
☐ graphing	[ˈgræfɪŋ]	畫圖形的
☐ project	[ˈprɑdʒɛkt]	學校研究作業
☐ Physics	[ˈfɪzɪks]	物理學
☐ program	[ˈprogræm]	電腦程式
☐ show	[ʃo]	給……看
☐ calculator	[ˈkælkjəˌletɚ]	計算機
☐ scientific	[ˌsaɪənˈtɪfɪk]	科學的
☐ programming	[ˈprogræmɪŋ]	程式設計
☐ language	[ˈlæŋgwɪdʒ]	電腦語言
☐ complete	[kəmˈplit]	完成

MEMO

MEMO

國家圖書館出版品預行編目資料

躺著學美語會話1000 / 張瑪麗, Willy Roberts合著. -- 新
北市：哈福企業, 2020.08
面 ；　公分. -- (英語系列；64)

ISBN 978-986-99161-3-4(平裝附光碟片)

1.英語 2.會話

805.188　　　　　　　　　　109011123

英語系列 : 64

躺著學美語會話1000

合著／ 張瑪麗 , Willy Roberts
出版者／哈福企業有限公司
地址／新北市板橋區五權街 16 號 1 樓
電話／ (02) 2808-4587 傳真／ (02) 2808-6545
郵政劃撥／ 31598840 　戶名／哈福企業有限公司
出版日期／ 2020 年 8 月
定價／ NT$ 320 元 (附 MP3)

全球華文國際市場總代理／采舍國際有限公司
地址／新北市中和區中山路 2 段 366 巷 10 號 3 樓
電話／ (02) 8245-8786 　傳真／ (02) 8245-8718
網址／ www.silkbook.com 　新絲路華文網

香港澳門總經銷／和平圖書有限公司
地址／香港柴灣嘉業街 12 號百樂門大廈 17 樓
電話／ (852) 2804-6687 　傳真／ (852) 2804-6409
定價／港幣 107 元 (附 MP3)

封面內頁圖片取材自／ shutterstock
email ／ welike8686@Gmail.com
網址／ Haa-net.com
facebook ／ Haa-net 哈福網路商城

哈福

哈福